ON THE FENCE

A Chimney Creek Romance by

Emily Conrad

one

. . .

THE BARKING REACHED a fever pitch that echoed through the lush peace of early summer in Chimney Creek, Wisconsin.

As the sole veterinarian in her small town, Morgan Reynolds knew all the dogs who lived nearby. The sound seemed to emanate from her own backyard, but no one in her immediate vicinity owned a dog large enough to make this deep-throated racket. Grasping her mail in one hand, she glanced at the sold sign in her neighbor's front yard.

She hadn't seen a dog when the man moved in yesterday, but that didn't mean he didn't own one. She hustled up her driveway and let herself into her fenced backyard. From there, she could scan the neighboring properties for the unhappy canine.

One step inside the waist-high fence, she froze.

About six feet on the wrong side of the fence—*inside* her yard—a large, white dog half crouched, barking wildly. Looked to her like a white shepherd, though not a purebred.

The dog aimed his frustration at her toppled grill, which lay a few feet from him, the grate and charcoal in the grass. He could easily get burned, if he hadn't already.

And where were the drumsticks she'd left to cook while checking the mail?

A cord attached to the dog's collar indicated his route like a dotted line following a character through a comic strip. The line circled the legs of the grill before disappearing over the fence. He must've smelled the meat and jumped over to investigate. Had he pulled that cord right off his owner's house?

If this guy had eaten all her chicken, surgery could be in his future. She'd had to operate on dogs who'd ingested less. But to determine the extent of the problem, she first needed to calm him down. Without getting bit.

With a prayer for help, she laid the mail on the patio table and eased closer.

Though his head bobbed with each frantic bark, she made out his roughly cropped ears. The crude alteration suggested someone had tried to make this dog a fighter.

Had they succeeded?

A shape moved on the other side of her white lattice fence.

With a hand braced on the top rail, a man cleared the three-foot barrier with the ease of an athlete. His running shoes landed in the mulch of her flower bed.

"Dax." He spoke with confident intensity.

The dog hushed, straightened, and looked from the grill to the newcomer with a tail wag that meant the animal thought all his problems were now solved.

Morgan's were just beginning because this pair of fence jumpers had to be her new neighbors.

When the real estate agent told her with a wink that an attractive "bachelor" had purchased the house next door, she assumed seventy-year-old Vanna's idea of good looks wouldn't match her own. She'd assumed wrong, if this blue-eyed, brown-haired, square-faced man was Mr. Bachelor. Now if only he hadn't left a dog unattended and poorly restrained. And was he responsible for those ears?

In precise movements, the man unclipped Dax from the useless tie-out. Though now loose, the canine stayed by his owner's side as the man righted the grill and pulled the cord from around the metal legs. His snug T-shirt followed his every move even more closely than Dax's watchful gaze. The evening sun cast a shadow from his triceps as he pointed to the fence. "Go on home."

Dax rotated his head sideways, the picture of confusion.

"Go on. Out." He motioned, and the dog trotted into the flower bed, paused as if to ask if he must, then sprung over the fence from a standstill.

The movement jolted Morgan from her amazement. "Wait. I need to examine him."

As if Dax understood, he sat on the opposite side of the fence. One word from his master, and he'd pop back over.

"Examine him?" The man turned to face her. For an instant, his expression showed only incredulity, like she'd suggested launching the dog into space. Then his gaze landed on her. His mouth opened with surprise and he crossed his arms. "You've got to be kidding."

Her sloppy ponytail brushed her neck as she glanced down. She hadn't caught a glimpse in a mirror lately, but by this time of day, most of her makeup had usually worn off. But most likely, the man's annoyance stemmed from her scrubs. Between the kitten pattern covering her outfit and her desire to examine Dax, he might have guessed her profession and was cursing his luck for having moved in next door to a veterinarian.

She forced her shoulders back, mirroring his confidence as best she could. "He ate four chicken drumsticks. Do you know how bad chicken bones are for dogs?"

The guy had the nerve to wave her off. "He's eaten worse." His ice-blue eyes fixed on her. Waiting for her to back down.

There was something uncanny about this man. His eyes,

especially, reminded her of someone. A kid, but from where? A TV show?

She blinked. Diverted her energy to the real problem. "You shouldn't leave him unattended like that."

The man's jaw ticked. "I'm sorry he jumped the fence. I only stepped inside to get food." He motioned toward the house next door. A plate of steaks rested on a plastic storage chest by the side entrance. "The tie-out came with the house. I didn't know it was loose."

She repressed a lecture about verifying such things. "What happened to his ears?"

"He's a rescue." His clipped tone warned Morgan that he'd recognized her underlying suspicion—that he'd cropped them himself—and that she'd crossed a line.

Fair enough. "You're the new neighbor."

With that serious expression, Mr. Bachelor's face could make the cover of one of those romantic suspense novels Callie, one of her vet techs, was always reading. Maybe that was why he looked familiar; he fit a type. "Would've thought you'd have picked that up spying yesterday."

"Spying?"

"From the garage."

"I *saw*, but I wasn't spying." She certainly hadn't stared long enough to figure out which man owned the place out of the stream of guys moving boxes and furniture. "It was a busy day for both of us. I figured we'd meet soon enough. I just didn't think it'd be under these circumstances."

Mr. Bachelor smirked. "Maybe if you'd brought us a casserole like a friendly neighbor, Dax wouldn't have had to take matters into his own hands."

"You obviously have food." She motioned at the steaks. "It's your responsibility to keep your mutt off mine."

The statement sounded incredibly sharp. Rude, even. She never called dogs mutts—she actually preferred mixed breeds to purebreds and their hereditary health issues. Even her own dogs were rescues without pedigrees. And it wasn't like this situation was the dog's fault.

But instead of bristling, Mr. Bachelor laughed and stepped back into the flower bed. Dax danced eagerly, excited to have his master back.

Breach of civility aside . . . "He really ought to see a vet. I—"

Mr. Bachelor hopped the fence, swept the plate of steaks up, and yanked open his side door. "Come on, Dax."

They disappeared inside.

Well.

She pressed her lips together.

Honestly, yes, she should've gone and introduced herself yesterday. The close-knit community was one of her favorite parts of this small community in northwestern Wisconsin. And that comment about mutts had been rude.

But she hated change and surprises, and a troublesome new neighbor brought both, as if all her plans weren't already in upheaval. How much more did the Lord think she could take?

———

As he cooked his steaks under the broiler, Hale Bastian paced.

She hadn't said as much, but *you're a dog abuser* had been written all over her face, and that bothered him. Not because she was pretty or because he felt guilty for Dax's chicken heist —though she was, and he did—but because he knew Morgan Reynolds. Mistaking him for the sort of man who'd mistreat animals rubbed salt in the wound of her failure to recognize him.

Twenty years had passed since they'd seen each other. Morgan had grown taller and thinned out since the summer he'd left. The fiery red of her hair had mellowed to copper. Her face, too, had matured, but he still knew the open planes of her cheeks and forehead, her straight and narrow nose. He'd have recognized her even in the most unexpected places —a crowded airport, the streets of Iraq, anywhere.

But for him? Nothing. She hadn't shown the slightest flicker of recognition, even though they stood just a mile or two from where they'd spent years as an unlikely pair of best friends.

In her defense, his thirteen-year-old self had worn braces and glasses, and his hair half hid his ears. Plus, he'd been shorter than her by the inch she'd lorded over him whenever she'd had the chance. Now, he had a couple of inches on her and the muscle mass to go with it. Not to mention a few brutal experiences that had aged him in ways that went beyond the physical. Still. Her complete unawareness of his identity reopened the sting of their falling out two decades ago, when he'd learned the hard way that she meant more to him than he ever meant to her.

He never would've purchased this house if he'd known she lived just across the property line.

He rubbed his face and groaned. "Twenty years."

Dax kept his nose angled toward the oven, but his brown eyes switched their focus to Hale as if to say that by now, bygones should be bygones. He agreed. They'd been kids, really. Teenagers, maybe, but only as a technicality. They'd since grown into bona fide adults, yet they'd both reverted into moody adolescents during that reintroduction.

He curled his fingers. Two golden retrievers had trotted around in her yard earlier. It was a wonder those two hadn't escaped that joke of a fence long before Dax got to it.

"Good fences make good neighbors, Morgan."

Dax spared him another look.

Hale pointed at him. "This is your fault."

Two innocent brown eyes blinked at him.

"Okay, but you didn't help."

Dax licked his chops and returned his focus to the oven.

The dog couldn't understand that the offensive he'd launched against the neighbor undermined everything Hale had moved here to reclaim.

Chimney Creek had been the most peaceful part of his life. As he'd prayed the Lord would lead him to green pastures, he'd felt certain of the nudge to return. But if he was going to enjoy green pastures here, he needed to make peace with Morgan.

After all, she didn't seem to have lost the stubborn, bold streak that had made them fast friends as kids. Those same traits would make her a nuisance as an enemy. Especially if she lived directly next door. He should've asked more questions of his real estate agent, but really, what were the odds?

Chimney Creek was small, sure, but out of twenty thousand people, he shouldn't have been able to accidentally end up next to his former friend. He stilled. Unless, of course, God wanted it this way.

But for what purpose? To convey that Hale had misunderstood and shouldn't have come?

Or perhaps He just wanted Hale to get the uncomfortable part of this move over with right off the bat. Make peace with the friend who'd snubbed him all those years ago, since it seemed he still harbored a grudge against her.

The savory aroma of roasting meat curled into the kitchen. Fine. He would attempt to negotiate a cease-fire by taking one of these steaks to her.

As the meat rested, he prepped baked potatoes and steamed vegetables. Since he still hadn't located his real dinnerware, he filled a paper plate and wrapped it in foil. With Dax in his kennel to protect Hale's dinner, he stepped into the mild June evening and carried a second plate next door.

When he knocked on the front door, the dogs barked. Through the window, he watched a cat scamper from a sunny spot. Like her aunt Dorie, the town veterinarian, Morgan had always loved animals. Figured she'd share her home with a bunch of them as an adult.

She appeared behind the storm door. Frowning, she inched it open. She must've redone her ponytail since he'd seen her in the yard, because the wisps of red hair that had framed her face were now pulled back.

He lifted the plate. "We got off on the wrong foot. Consider this my apology for Dax eating your dinner."

Twin dents appeared over the inner edge of her eyebrows, like they used to when she was leery as a kid. Like the time he'd told her astronauts lived on the moon, or later, when he'd said he wasn't scared to move away from Chimney Creek.

She accepted the offering, and the foil crinkled as she lifted an edge. Steam puffed toward her face. When she folded the covering back in place, her blue irises focused on him. "Thanks."

She used to tell him she was jealous of his eye color, but he'd always appreciated her medium blue, flecked with dark blue and gray in a combination that was uniquely hers.

Years had passed—more years than they'd known each other in the first place. How could he still so clearly see in her the girl he'd once known? And what did it mean that she didn't seem to recognize him?

"About your dog—"

He held up a hand to stop her. "He'll stay out of your yard."

"But chicken bones—"

He retreated another step. She had no idea who she was dealing with. On so many levels.

"He'll be okay. I have an appointment to get to, though, so. . ." As he edged off her porch, the marks above her eyebrows returned.

Her skepticism made sense. He was dressed for a run, and six p.m. might be late for most appointments, but that's when the lady at the animal shelter told him to come by to get set up as a volunteer. After a breath, he changed his mind about telling her where he was headed.

Given her reaction to Dax's adventure tonight, she wouldn't want Hale interacting with other animals. But Dax was fine, and Hale had moved here despite Morgan, not because of her.

two

. . .

THE ANIMAL SHELTER stood on a small rise. Stretching farm fields surrounded the cinderblock building. When Hale came here as a kid with Morgan and her aunt Dorie, he'd only seen the good.

Way out here, he couldn't hear his parents fighting, and he'd been surrounded by dogs. All different sizes, shapes, and energy levels with wagging tails and friendly tongues. In retrospect, Dorie probably put special care into choosing which dogs to set loose in the play area with him and Morgan. And it'd probably been four canines at a time, rather than the dozen his memory told him he'd run around with.

The animal shelter had been his favorite place, literally in the middle of green pastures. Or farm fields, anyway.

He snorted at the memory of Morgan as a girl, retreating onto a bench in the yard each time the dogs bounded out to them. He used to stand in front of her, greeting the animals and distracting them from her until they'd calmed down.

He'd been happy to be her protector, and she'd been happy for his help—until the time he teased her for her fear in front of their classmates. She'd stopped talking to him for two days. He apologized in the most dramatic fashion his ten-year-old brain could muster—taping a sign that said *I'm sorry* to her bedroom window. When she forgave him, he never sided against her again.

Funny how, now, even their rough patches were part of the good old days.

But memory did all kinds of favors, if the animal shelter was any indication. As he drove up, the building was about half the size he remembered. The tan cinderblock would've blended right into the Iraqi desert.

He drew a breath and exhaled. He wasn't a child anymore. He didn't see with a child's eyes, and nothing was perfect. But some places were peaceful and good, and even if he couldn't see through childlike innocence anymore, he could appreciate the good things.

The Chimney Creek Animal Shelter was one of the best of those.

Mature trees shaded the property, including the exercise runs that protruded from the back of the building. Dogs bounced in the small, fenced areas. As he got closer, their barks carried over the crackle of his tires on the gravel road.

The drive ended in a dirt lot at the front of the building. He parked, locked the vehicle, and scanned the exterior once more. The place couldn't be much larger than his house. Up close, the tan paint could use a refresh.

The shelter's glass door was clean, except for a couple of nose prints at knee-level. As he stepped inside, the likely culprit trotted up to him. He bent to scratch the Sheltie behind the ears.

"Can I help you?" From behind the reception desk, a woman in a green polo blinked at him through rimless glasses. She had her hair back in a bun so tight she had to have a headache, but she met his look with a smile.

Beside her stood two older ladies. The one with silver hair might be around retirement age. The other, with pure white hair and papery skin, seemed another generation older. She held a kitten in what looked like an attempt to rub noses, apparently oblivious to his arrival.

Her companion, who also held a furball, tapped her shoulder without breaking her stare at Hale. "Edie." When the woman didn't lower her cat or turn toward them, her friend put more force into the taps. "Edie!"

Edie lowered the kitten, turned, and finally spotted him. "Oh."

They obviously didn't see many newcomers here. He chuckled. "I'm Hale Bastian. I called about helping out."

The younger lady in the green polo inhaled with pleasure. "Wonderful that you moved here and signed right up." She bent her arm and swung her fist in the cheesiest show of enthusiasm he'd seen in a long time. "You must love animals."

His history with this place would raise a slew of questions he had no desire to answer. "I believe in rescues."

The lady grinned. "You'll fit right in. And just wait till you meet the local vet."

He was curious how that reunion would go. Dorie Reynold's clinic had appeared completely unchanged when he'd driven by. What would she say to him after all these years?

He refocused. "I didn't catch your name."

She laid her finger on her polo, where script partially answered his question. "Mili. McFarden."

He'd had a McFarden in his classes as a kid. Not Mili, though. Must've been one of her siblings.

Mili motioned to the women next to her. "Eileen and Edie volunteer here."

"What, dear?" Edie asked.

"You volunteer here," Mili shouted.

"Oh, yes." Edie flashed him a smile.

Eileen studied him with interest that seemed a little too

keen, as if she might hope to set him up with a single relative. Time to get moving.

"How about the grand tour?" he asked. "And if you've got a dog with extra energy, I could use a run myself." No better way to shed the stress of his reunion with Morgan.

"Sure." Mili rounded the counter. "There's a lab mix who could use some love. Come with me."

The first stop on the tour featured a cat room, where at least a dozen felines lounged on various climbing structures. Mili swooped up the closest one and rubbed three fingers over the cat's forehead, eliciting an instant purr. "These are the adoptable cats, all healthy and ready to go. Given we might have to close this fall, it'd be nice to see more going to homes than coming in, but it is kitten season." She lifted her eyebrows on the last two words, as if those were the most important.

"What happens this fall? Renovations?" A contractor himself, he'd love to give the place an overhaul. Update the wood-paneled reception area, replace the fifty-year-old laminate, make other adjustments to suit the needs of staff and animals.

She stiffened. "Ah, no."

His heart sank, but instead of expounding on the situation, she continued the tour.

The next room held cabinets, a wheeled examination table, and a grooming station. She rested her hands on the exam table. "Mostly, we use the grooming station with new intakes. Dr. Reynolds takes care of vaccinations and other routine needs right on site." She pointed to a tower of cages in the corner. "These are the cats with dietary restrictions. Adoptable, but they'll need to go to a home that can accommodate."

He crossed his arms as trepidation prickled his skin. The longer she attempted to distract him, the worse he imagined the problems. "Why might you close this fall?"

Mili's shoulders dropped. "I shouldn't have mentioned it,

but it's been weighing on me. I haven't said anything to the others. They're more invested, you know? But since you're new, maybe it just seemed like I could tell you without breaking your heart the way it would for them. Maybe you deserved the warning not to get too attached."

Too late for that. Still, she hadn't answered his question, and he couldn't attack a problem he couldn't define. "This place is closing permanently."

"Maybe. We operate on a deficit every year. A lot of independent shelters like us do, despite grants and fundraising and donations. But for us, it's gotten to the point where, if we don't suddenly raise an unprecedented amount, we'll be forced to shut our doors. Chimney Creek is a small town. Maybe too small to support a shelter, though, well, obviously . . ." Her nose twitched, as if warding off tears. She motioned to the cats lounging in their cages. "We provide necessary services, but everything costs something."

He nodded once. "How much do you need?"

She named the number on a sigh, a breezy way to announce a hefty amount.

Raising so much over one summer did sound unlikely.

"But keep it to yourself, okay? For now? I still haven't figured out how to tell everyone."

"I'll let you tell them." Except, as soon as the promise was out, he wondered if Morgan and Dorie knew. They loved this place as much as he did. As soon as they found out, the pair would find a way to raise the funds, wouldn't they? Dorie Reynolds had been kind but not soft. She'd fight for what she wanted, and no doubt Morgan would as well.

Mili escorted him to the kennels. Many of the pens held two or three dogs, almost all of whom barked at the sight of them. "We rotate them outdoors for a little while each day," she shouted over the racket. "And volunteers help make sure they each get some exercise, whether it's fetch or a walk."

"They're all adoptable?" Even as he asked, his brain worked elsewhere, on the problem of fundraising.

"We have a few strays who haven't been here long enough yet. Our first goal is to reunite them with their owners." She stopped at the end of the row of kennels and looked through the chain link. A sleek, massive dog, possibly a purebred Rottweiler, shied away from their presence and sat in the back corner of his kennel, tail tucked and back curved protectively. "Samson here arrived two days ago, and his owner hasn't come out of the woodwork. In his case, that might be best because he has extreme fear issues that suggest abuse. I'm worried for him. Even if we do all the rehabilitation we can, he still might not be adoptable by the time we have to close. That would not spell good news for him."

Hale squatted, putting himself at eye level with the animal. "What's his story?"

"One day they found him hanging out by Hank's Convenience . . ." She hesitated as if to ask if he knew the place.

He bobbed his head. To buy candy, he used to walk to the store, located on the five-way intersection in downtown Chimney Creek known as The Corners. Hank's Convenience was owned by a well-known local family, the Fieldings. Some of their kids were adopted, some biological, but Hale had been jealous of them all because their parents had been so involved and caring. A stark contrast to his own rocky home life.

"Samson was scavenging through garbage cans and growling when anyone tried to get close. Hank called us, and we picked him up—though not without some difficulty. Samson is the name we gave him. He didn't have a collar or a microchip, so unless his owners come to us, we may never know his whole story."

Down the hall, a particularly insistent dog continued a string of barks. The others let out occasional yaps. Samson lurked silently in the corner of his kennel, hunched like a gargoyle as his eyes shifted from Hale to Mili and back again. Hale touched the back of his hand to the fencing, but the dog's nose didn't even quiver with curiosity.

"Don't feel bad," Mili said. "He won't let anyone close."

Hale had won Dax over with food. If they'd first met when he had nothing to offer, Dax might've stared at him from a distance too. Still, there were differences between the dogs. Dax had been scrappy and unbeaten by his circumstances, despite having been on his own. Meanwhile, Samson moped and cowered. An animal his size would be dangerous if not rehabilitated well.

"Do any trainers volunteer their time here?"

"One, but she can't come every day, which is what this guy needs to establish trust with someone. We'll work with him, but we're pulled in about a million different directions. No breakthroughs yet, and unfortunately, the clock is ticking."

"You mind if I see what I can do? I'll even cover the cost of his supplies so he's not a burden if it takes longer than usual to make him ready for adoption."

"We won't turn down the help. Although . . ." She held one finger near her ear. "That crazy barker is Russ, insisting on the exercise I promised him when you agreed to come tonight."

He straightened, watching Samson, whose gaze followed his every move. Maybe Hale hadn't shown it as obviously as this dog, but after two tours, he'd struggled to reintegrate into normal life too. If he could help an animal past trauma and into a peaceful future, he'd do it.

Especially if this place would no longer be around in a couple of months.

He scanned the surroundings. Though smaller than he'd remembered, the important things remained the same.

The dogs' promise of fun and companionship.

The sense that he belonged here.

He couldn't let the shelter close. "What's all the money for? I'm a contractor, and I'd be happy to donate my time to repairs, if that's the issue." He had a full slate of bathroom and kitchen renovations lined up, but he'd fit in the extra responsibility. It wasn't like he had a social life here. "I can't do everything, but I could make a dent."

"Do you do foundation and heating and cooling work?"

His hopes fell. The jobs he could do wouldn't help much if they couldn't keep the temperature or the building itself stabilized. He'd had connections in both lines of work before he moved, but none this far north. "No, I'm a general contractor."

"Anyway, it's not all building maintenance. Supplies. Veterinary costs. The list goes on and on."

"What kind of fundraising do you guys do?"

"Our biggest event is the annual dog walk. That's coming up in August. We're staying open until then, holding out hope people will be more generous than usual, but . . ." She puffed up her cheeks and blew out the air. "Honestly, they're always generous. I don't know that we can really expect the same people to somehow come up with so much more than usual."

"Maybe we need to make the event appeal to more than just the people of Chimney Creek. Back where I'm from, a car dealership did one of those contests where dogs jump as far as they can off a dock into water. They had this big, long pool set up in their parking lot for the competition. That's just one event. You could add a whole bunch. With enough going on, you could draw more people, and more people would mean more donations. Plus, you could charge people to enter the contests and get a cut of vendor sales."

Her face brightened. "I'll sign you up for the fundraising committee. We could use fresh ideas."

"Do that."

Mili clapped. "Great. We meet at the library. I'll double-check the date and time for the next one and text you."

"I'll be there."

Samson stood, but instead of approaching the gate, he turned a nervous circle and plopped to his haunches again. Poor guy.

If Hale had his way, not only would the shelter continue its mission in Chimney Creek, but Samson would also make a great companion someday. Hale might adopt him himself. Morgan would hate that, another dog who could easily hop her ridiculous little fence.

Smiling at the thought, he followed Mili to the leashes.

three

. . .

THE DAY after the chicken incident, Morgan watched Violet and Rose, her golden retrievers, chase each other around the perimeter of the yard. Dark clouds to match the forecast loomed to the west, but the setting sun dropped below them at the horizon, sending dramatic golden light across the landscape.

Two soft plops sounded to her left. She turned to find Dax with his front paws on the top rail of her fence. His sweet brown eyes peered at her, a dark contrast to his white fur.

Yesterday she worried that he'd been subjected to dog fighting at some point, but he watched her girls play with a curious, relaxed posture. And then looked at her again.

"I don't have any more chicken for you." She did have some choice words for Dax's owner, though.

Mr. Bachelor had attached a new tie-out to the house, one just long enough for Dax to perch his front paws on the ledge without getting over. Such a precise length—long enough to look but not long enough to jump—had to have been purposeful.

Well, fine. If that was the relationship he wanted, she didn't have to worry about frustrating him either—and he was nowhere to be seen at the moment. She could check Dax over to ensure he hadn't burned his paws or mouth and that his belly wasn't causing him pain.

Her trip to the fence drew Rose and Violet, who finally spotted the newcomer and zoomed up to greet him. Dax dropped from his perch, and the three sniffed loudly through the lattice. No growls. Only a couple of short, low-level barks, as if they were tossing casual hellos to each other.

That answered the question about whether Dax had learned to fight.

Despite the barks, the side door of the neighboring house remained closed. Mr. Bachelor either hadn't heard or didn't care. Probably the latter.

The leafy branches of her hydrangea bush, still a month or more from blooming, brushed her pant leg as she rested her hands on the fence. The neighbor had hopped over, but Morgan couldn't envision swinging her feet to waist height in one fluid movement like that. She scooted her hip onto the board that topped the fence, then pivoted to swing her feet over. Her left heel hit the rail. She wobbled but managed to land on her feet in the neighbor's yard.

Dax barked a greeting, brandishing his tail the way the baton girls swirled flags in the Memorial Day parade. He accepted her attention playfully, wiggling and hopping as she ran her hands over him. A tawny cream color tipped his white fur across his back and shoulders. He didn't react as though his belly felt tender or painful. She saw no marks on the pads of his front paws. And in the quick glimpses she had of his mouth, he didn't appear to have any burns from the grill.

She scratched under his chin with both hands. "You lucked out this time, but you need to take better care of yourself, okay?"

Dax slurped his tongue across her cheek.

"Satisfied?" a deep voice asked.

Her attention snapped up.

The neighbor's detached garage stood twenty feet off, taking up a large portion of the backyard. The garage door was open, but she hadn't heard any noise to lead her to believe someone was inside. Yet Mr. Bachelor leaned against the siding a foot or two from the opening, arms crossed and chin lifted.

"I'm a vet." Who was trespassing. Her face blazed.

The man's eyebrows lifted, and the sunlight cut across his features. "Really?"

"Why would that surprise you?"

He lifted one shoulder and shook his head lightly. He uncrossed his arms and wiped his hand on a rag she hadn't noticed in his grip sooner. Judging by the grease he smeared on the white cloth, he'd been working on something mechanical in the garage.

Handsome, athletic, and capable of fixing things?

Didn't matter. Her plans did not involve dating. Especially not a wildcard like this guy. She couldn't control who God allowed to move in next door—or a gazillion other things for that matter—but she could control her focus. Her work ethic. Her to-do list.

She fell back on the questions she would ask if he'd brought Dax to her clinic. "Has he been eating and drinking?"

"Yes, ma'am." He continued studying her in that unnerving way of his, like he had a secret he was daring her to unearth. "How was the steak last night?"

"Not bad." Actually, it'd been excellent. She rarely sprang for the expense, and even if she did, she never managed to cook it to perfection the way Mr. Bachelor had.

He dipped his head toward Violet and Rose. "Your dogs are also big enough to hop your fence. Probably more easily than you did just now."

Embarrassment drove her gaze away from him to her own

yard. Violet rolled in the grass. Rose sniffed along the foundation of the garage. "They would never."

He whistled, and Dax met him halfway to his side door. He flipped the rag over his shoulder, freeing up his hands to give his dog some attention. "Properly motivated, they might surprise you."

Properly motivated? Was he threatening to bait her dogs with steak?

If Mr. Bachelor bribed her dogs into jumping her fence, she could train Dax to . . .

Freeze right there. What about this man brought out this side of her?

She was not going to use a dog as a pawn in a neighborhood battle of wills.

Okay. Maybe a little bit. "We're supposed to get bad weather tonight. How does he do with thunderstorms?"

"Terrible." He straightened, and only then did she see the hint of a smile. "Hides under the bed, and if the sirens go off, he insists we wait in a corner of the basement with our heads covered." He covered his head, mimicking the tornado drill pose she'd been taught in kindergarten. As he lifted his arms, his biceps flexed. The show of strength had been inadvertent, she was almost positive, but his teasing smirk told her he was more likely to go outside to look for tornadoes than to duck for cover.

"Okay, tough guy. Some dogs get scared by loud noises. Compassionate owners look for ways to help their animals cope." The words escaped before she filtered them with her better sense.

Maybe Mr. Bachelor brought out this kind of response from a lot of people, because he took it in stride, still smiling. "Don't worry. Dax and I know how to look out for each other. Been doing it a long time now."

Looking out for each other? Was Dax a service dog?

Mr. Bachelor could obviously see and had the opposite of

mobility issues. But a dog could help with a variety of tasks from monitoring blood sugar, predicting seizures, and managing PTSD. The only way to know if Dax helped with anything like that would be to ask, at which point, Mr. Bachelor would be well within his rights to tell her to mind her own business.

"What is it you do?" she asked.

"I'm a contractor. Kitchen and bath remodels. Additions."

"Who do you work for?" Chimney Creek was pretty small. Not small enough that she knew everyone, but she did treat the local carpenter's dog.

"Myself."

"Oh." It took guts to try to build a business from scratch directly upon moving to town. She glanced toward the street. Would anyone here trust a newcomer enough to hire him?

"I'm licensed and insured, and I come with great references." Tiny creases formed by his eyes with his smile. "I lined up a few months of work before moving here."

He ought to add mind reading to his list of specialties. How had he known she was doubting his business sense? Only once she forced a smile did she realize she'd been scowling. Maybe that had been his hint.

"I hope it goes well." She waved.

He watched her with amusement, waiting for her next move like he thought her fussy and silly. Which she was. At least around this guy.

She looked the way she'd come, but she wouldn't attempt to navigate the fence again with him watching. She'd have to go around the front of the house and through the gate. Blades of grass popped as she pivoted on her heel.

A whistle sliced the air. Hale braced a hand on Brady's back, meaning to get them both to safety, but an explosion rocked the ground, the air. For a weightless moment, he felt himself suspended by the blast.

The explosion woke him.

Another whistle.

No. Not a whistle. A whine.

Light flickered through Hale's bedroom, emanating from the window. The storms Morgan had warned him of had arrived, bringing with them nearly constant thunder and lightning.

Something cold and wet nudged his forearm. Dax sat beside his bed, his head on the mattress, as close to Hale as he could get without breaking the ban on dogs in the bed.

Hale slid from under the covers and sank to the rug beside the canine. A deep breath slowed his heart rate. A few years ago, he would've woken drenched in sweat, shouting, and believing himself back in combat. Now, the sensations didn't come on as strong or leave him as shaken.

Still, a war zone wasn't a place he cared to revisit, even in a dream.

Dax laid his warm, broad head on Hale's thigh. Had the dog understood the danger over in Iraq? Did he understand the difference between the noise of thunder and that of gunfire and mortar rounds?

He rubbed his hand down Dax's back, over the snug wrap that supposedly helped dogs feel safe. Though they used it for thunderstorms and the Fourth of July, Dax still whined and paced when the racket started. He wasn't a service dog, but his nervous habit had pulled Hale from more than one bad dream over the years. The least he could do was try to help Dax cope too.

Whether Morgan believed it or not, he had a heart.

He sighed. So she'd followed her aunt into veterinary medicine. Good for her. She'd always loved animals, and her aunt was likely grooming her to take over her practice.

The rightness of it, the rhythm of one generation setting

up the next for success fit the image of Chimney Creek that had drawn him back here.

After coming home from his time in the service, he'd found peace elusive. Dax, time, and therapy helped. But still, something was missing. Had been since long before he'd shipped out overseas, actually. As far back as his parents' arguments in his childhood, he'd grown accustomed to fighting.

The spat with Morgan showed a man could change his address but still carry around the same old habits. He was a fighter, and no matter how hard he looked, he wouldn't find the green pastures mentioned in Psalm 23 unless God Himself showed him the way.

He'd hoped the nudge to come to Chimney Creek had been just that—God, showing him the way—but he couldn't be sure. Not yet. Not with how he'd immediately started a war with Morgan, who still hadn't recognized him.

"Come on, Dax." He climbed to his feet and led the way to the living room.

He put in a movie meant to drown out the noise of the storm and allowed Dax to join him on the couch. He didn't care to examine the choice closely enough to determine whether he was helping himself or the dog. Either way, the arrangement usually had them both back asleep long before the movie—or the storm—ended.

four

. . .

THREE OTHER VEHICLES occupied the shelter parking lot as Morgan edged her sedan into an empty space. Hopefully that meant someone was here to adopt one of the animals.

When Morgan had stopped to check on some of the animals under her care last week, a few days after Mr. Bachelor moved in, Mili had mentioned that the annual fundraising walk would be an important source of donations this year. Since that was true every year and Mili seemed more stressed than usual, Morgan guessed they needed a little more than normal.

Lord, please show us how to bring in the funds we need. So many of Your creatures depend on this place.

They'd raise the money. They had to, and thankfully, they had a tried-and-true plan, thanks to Aunt Dorie. Just thinking about the spreadsheets and copious notes on running a successful dog walk fundraiser lowered her heart rate.

Inside, eighty-six-year-old Edie Gable sat behind the reception counter next to sixty-something Eileen Jonas, a waitress who always meant well but didn't seem to recognize her gossip habit for what it was. The pair of volunteers stuffed envelopes for a mail campaign.

"Hello, ladies." Morgan spoke loudly enough that even hard-of-hearing Edie looked up from her work. Morgan needed to check some paperwork in the office beyond them, so she stepped behind the counter.

Eileen swiped a damp sponge over a flap, pressed it closed, and dropped the letter in the box, then swiveled her chair toward Morgan. "Have you met the new volunteer?"

She shook her head. As far as she knew, there hadn't been any new helpers recently. Perhaps a college student, home for the summer, had offered to help out.

"We think he's a secret agent!" If any secret agents *were* in the building, Edie's shout would've warned them their cover had been blown.

"It's the way he carries himself." Eileen wiggled her fingers as if to grasp a slippery concept. "Economy of movement."

"And you should see him run!"

How had these two made some poor volunteer run? Morgan didn't bother to hide her grin. "Do secret agents run differently than everyone else?"

"He runs like the assassin in that movie—you know, with his hands completely straight." Eileen mimed the movement. "It's like he's on a mission."

"He's also very quiet." Edie lowered her voice to normal volume, probably meaning to whisper. "I went in back with a new chore sheet for the dog kennel area, and I turned around, and there he was. Right behind me."

Morgan looked to Eileen, who had excellent hearing, expecting her to minimize this last observation, but instead the woman nodded. "We were both working right here one day, and we planned to leave when he did so we could, you know . . ." Eileen moved two fingers to indicate a person walking.

Morgan suppressed a laugh. "Follow him?"

Eileen gave a noncommittal shrug. "We didn't get to because we didn't even know he'd passed us on his way out until we heard the bells on the door. But when we do see him, he's very intense around the eyes."

Morgan should probably not indulge this line of thinking, but she could use the mood boost. "What would a secret agent be doing in Chimney Creek?"

"Who knows. And of course we don't know he *is* a secret agent." Eileen spoke loudly, probably for Edie's benefit. "It's just that there's something about him. More than meets the eye. He's a man with secrets."

"And a past!" Edie chimed in.

"Okay, well if that's true, be careful, you two." Still chuckling, she let herself into the office, where Mili sat at a paper-cluttered desk. "I hear there's a new volunteer."

"My theories aren't as extreme as some, but he is a little evasive about personal questions." Mili adjusted her glasses. "Whatever the case, he's been very dedicated to Samson. So if he *is* a secret agent, he's one of the good guys." She handed over a file folder.

Morgan scanned the paperwork inside. "Lots to do today."

"Always." Mili turned back to the spreadsheet on her computer screen. "Give me a few minutes, and I'll help you herd cats."

Morgan tucked the file under her arm and left the office, heart lighter than when she'd walked in. The goofy camaraderie of this place kept her going some days.

She dropped the file off in the exam room and checked on the cats there. By the time she finished, Mili joined her, and they administered vaccinations to the kittens who were due for them.

In addition to all those that had been in the shelter's care the last time Morgan had been in, another dozen kitties now waited for vaccinations and adoptions.

"How are we going to find homes for all of these?" Mili lifted a pint-sized calico and set her in the open-top cardboard box they used to carry litters from one room to another.

"Two at a time." Morgan set two other kittens in, then grabbed a third who was investigating the edge of the exam table. Since young cats seemed to do better with a playmate, the shelter had a policy of adopting them out in pairs. While that meant finding half the homes, it also didn't appeal to some potential adopters.

Mili rounded up the last of the litter. "On the positive side, the new volunteer has lots of ideas."

Of course he did. All conversational roads led back to this newcomer today. As they worked together, Mili peppered her with stories of him. The new volunteer took three of the dogs for a two-mile run. The new volunteer spent half an hour sitting outside Samson's kennel each day. The new volunteer got soaked giving one of the dogs a bath.

Why was Mili so enamored with a high school or college student? She'd said the boy had just moved to town. Perhaps he had a cute, single father who'd piqued her interest.

Morgan had had her fill of newcomers lately, thank you very much.

Over the last week, she and her neighbor stuck to their own sides of the fence, but he, his muscles, and his snug-fitting T-shirts always seemed to be out in the yard when she was, Dax trotting along at his heels. He'd said he had jobs lined up, but perhaps none of them had started yet. Or, perhaps, he left for work and returned all within the space of her workday. She did work long hours.

She opened the door of the exam room for Mili, whose hands were full with the box.

"I can introduce you now." The box tilted, and Mili scrambled to adjust. Once she had the kittens balanced again, she scrunched her nose, lifting her glasses without touching them. "He should be here. He said he'd come to visit Samson during his lunch break now that he's working. It really is the cutest thing."

Could a high schooler break through to the beautiful dog? She hoped so. "Has Samson warmed to him yet?"

Mili tipped her head. "He's stopped going to the back corner, but he still won't come up to the gate. Unless I walk back there. Then he goes to the corner again."

"So if we go check up on them, we'll spook Samson." Morgan intended that to keep Mili from pursuing this.

"He's got to get used to us too." Mili settled the kittens into their enclosure. Once she'd latched the gate, she bustled back to the hall. "Just trust me."

Maybe if Morgan did as she asked, she wouldn't have to listen to a play-by-play of the new volunteer's actions the next time she came to care for the animals. She followed the shelter director to the dog kennels.

Barks bombarded them, as always. Morgan stepped close to the chain link and offered the back of her hand for the first kennel of dogs to sniff. "Hi, babies."

Before she could move on to the second kennel, she caught sight of the new volunteer, seated on the floor at the end of the row, his back against the gate of Samson's kennel. Like so many high schoolers seemed to constantly do, he had a phone in his hands—but he wasn't a high schooler at all. He was an all-too-familiar man in his thirties. Her neighbor.

Mr. Bachelor's eyes focused on Mili for only a second before his gaze fixed on Morgan. He lowered the phone and climbed to his feet. He wore dusty pants and boots suited to a construction site, and his T-shirt had seen better days.

She cleared her throat. "Am I going to see you everywhere now?"

He looked less surprised than she felt. Morgan had told him she was a vet, and Mili had likely been telling him about her, given all Morgan had heard of *the new volunteer* today. So he'd probably been prepared for this.

Unlike her.

"One of the perks of a small town," he said. "Though not the one I moved back here for."

Back?

Mili spun, looking between them. "You know each other?"

The man gave a tight smile. "Morgan and I go way back."

Way back to a week and a half ago. They'd never been formally introduced, and she still didn't know his name. He must've learned hers from Mili.

Asking for his name now would just raise more questions from the director and give him the pleasure of having knowledge about her that she didn't have about him. "He moved into the Jacobsons' old house. His dog promptly stole an entire package of chicken drumsticks off my grill."

Mili's round eyes matched the *O* shape her mouth made.

Morgan's throat sizzled with words of warning that he couldn't be trusted with shelter animals, given how poorly he supervised his own dog, but she wouldn't have that conversation in front of the man.

And Mili wanted him on the fundraising committee.

Morgan motioned her toward the hall. "A word?"

The director hesitated, gaze bouncing between them. "Okay, sure." She exited to the hall.

The volunteer pinned Morgan with an icy look as he sat back down at Samson's gate. Eileen had been right. He *was* intense around the eyes, and not just because of the shocking color of his irises.

Morgan held her tongue all the way out to the front desk in the foyer. Thankfully, Edie and Eileen had gone. "Can I see his volunteer application?"

Mili bit her lip and moved toward the desk.

"Did you call his references?"

"Yep." Mili unlocked and rolled open a file drawer, then

straightened with a packet of papers. "He's got a slew of personal and professional ones, and a few people around town have hired him for jobs. He started a kitchen remodel for Kerry and Fletch Johansson just today. He's here on his lunch break."

She accepted the paperwork. "People are too trusting. He might've come to town to swindle everyone."

"Swindle?" Mili snorted. "You're as bad as Edie and Eileen."

"Not all contractors are reputable." She turned her attention to the volunteer application.

Her vision stopped on the top line, where Mr. Bachelor had written his name.

Hale Bastian?

A memory played from years ago, warm breath brushing her thirteen-year-old lips, then the soft press of Hale's mouth against hers. A kiss had been the final item on his moving-away bucket list, one she never would've allowed if she hadn't been curious herself.

In retrospect, the kiss had been a peck—short, sweet, and honestly, a little damp. But in the moment, she'd felt that kiss all the way to her toes, and she'd hoped against hope that he put that milestone on his list because he liked her. When she got the miracle she'd been praying for and he stayed in Chimney Creek, the entire tone of their relationship would change. Childish adventures would be replaced by sweet gestures and cozy moments. They were thirteen and had their whole lives before them, and together they'd get to find out what that meant.

Except after the kiss, she didn't know how to act around him.

And then she got the opposite of a miracle. He left without saying goodbye.

Given the vividness of her memories, how had she not recognized him instantly? Especially considering those eyes.

Yet the loyal but scrawny boy she'd known was entirely different from the standoffish, athletic man back by the kennels.

"Are you okay?" Mili blinked behind her glasses, watching her as if she'd just delivered a terminal diagnosis.

"Yes." She choked the word out before noticing that she'd shaken her head no as she spoke.

Mili cringed. "He's been so wonderful with the dogs. I think if you just . . ."

She bit her lips.

Hale Bastian. Back after all this time. And if her experience with him as a neighbor was any indication, he wasn't much more considerate now than he'd been when he left in such a cruel way two decades ago.

"I need to get back to the office." She extended the application to Mili, though she couldn't look the woman in the eye.

When the paper lifted from her hand, she hurried out to her car and back to her clinic in downtown Chimney Creek. If only going home in the middle of the day were an option, but her schedule was packed.

Safely shut in her office, she pulled out her phone and selected Hannah from her contacts. If anyone could help her get her head back on straight in quick order, it was her oldest friend. The one she'd had since childhood. The one who'd listened to all the heartbreak when Hale ghosted her twenty years ago.

So, when Hannah answered, she forced out the words she still couldn't wrap her mind around.

"That new neighbor who's been annoying me since he moved in?"

Hannah chuckled. "The infamous Mr. Bachelor?"

"It's Hale Bastian. He lives right next door."

five

. . .

STILL SEATED outside Samson's kennel, Hale watched the door.

Somewhere out of his earshot, Morgan was probably ranting about how he shouldn't be involved with the shelter. In the ensuing conversation, Mili would spill his name. Hale couldn't imagine a scenario where that revelation would land him on Morgan's good side. He hadn't meant to keep his identity a secret, but, well . . . Morgan was the one who'd never bothered to ask his name.

The one who hadn't recognized him.

He rubbed his hand over his head, and his short hair ruffled between his fingers. He peered over his shoulder. Samson sat in the middle of his kennel, three feet closer than that first day.

Would Morgan have the gall and the pull to get Hale banned from the shelter?

If she did, he'd adapt. Morgan might hate him, but Mili loved him. Awkward, at times, but true. Even if the director caved and fired him from his unpaid position, she'd allow him to adopt the dog and continue rehabilitation.

His phone lit with his friend Brady's name and grinning profile picture.

He swiped the icon to answer the incoming call. "You're back?"

"Man, it was awesome." Brady's enthusiasm came through like a high five. "Can't make this stuff up. You've got to get in on this. You see the pictures?"

"I did." Hale studied the dingy cinderblock wall before him, a sad contrast to the beautiful mountainscapes Brady had led a group of hikers through. Hard to believe this was even the same world that boasted such serene vistas as what Brady had photographed.

But then, it was also the same world where he and Brady had served in the Middle East.

After their discharge, Hale wanted to make old things new and work with his hands, so he went back to school for a construction management degree. Brady started an adventure vacation company leading hikes through rainforests, mountains, and deserts on five continents.

"Had a lady complain about the cake I made on the last day, though. I mean, actual cake. We haven't seen civilization in days. I manage a feat like that, and she has the nerve to complain." Brady laughed. "But if you can get past the spoiled tourist stuff, this is the best job in the world."

"I'm glad, man. You deserve it."

"No, *you* do. If not for you . . . Look, what's the point in building someone's dream bathroom when you could be building your own dreams for once? Why did you choose a tiny town in backwoods Wisconsin over everything you could've had?"

Because Chimney Creek was where he'd once had everything. Here, he lived closer to better times and could rehabilitate houses and even a dog every now and then—assuming Morgan didn't put a stop to his volunteer work and he could save the shelter.

"You're thinking about it, aren't you?" Smug triumph laced Brady's voice.

Not exactly. "I'm committed to jobs through the end of the year."

"So after that?"

Hale laughed. "I bought a house. I'm not turning around and leaving."

"Houses sell. Life's short. The sooner you recognize and give up on mistakes, the more time you get for the good stuff. Don't tell me you've seen enough of the world."

Some parts of it, but he'd never tire of the parts of the world Brady's company frequented. "Tell you what. If this doesn't work out, you'll be my first call."

The door down the aisle opened, and the dogs erupted. Samson slunk to the back of his kennel. Mili stepped into the room, face awash in guilt.

"What is going on over there?" Brady's voice came through the phone, barely audible over the dogs. "Where are you?"

"At the animal shelter. I've got to go." He hung up and stood to face the verdict.

Mili stuck her hands in her pockets, then seemed to think better of it and threaded her fingers together. "I'm not even sure where to start."

"What'd Morgan say?"

She pursed her lips. "Not much. She took one look at your application, got all quiet and weird, and pretty much ran out of here."

"Huh." Not at all what he'd expected.

"You two know each other?"

"Knew. I grew up here. Left the summer before eighth grade."

"And now you live next door to her?"

He nodded.

Mili gave an exaggerated frown. Her long pause was likely a precursor to more questions he didn't want to answer.

He made a quick exit, but the sudden departure meant he arrived at the Johannson's house sooner than planned. Alex, the eighteen-year-old he'd hired to help dismantle the kitchen, hadn't returned from his own break yet. Hale let himself in through the back door to resume work.

Concern over whatever Morgan's next move would be meant today wasn't the worst day for demolition. If only he could take a sledgehammer to a wall the way they did on home makeover shows. Instead, he pried the doors off cabinets and left the discarded parts in a stack near the exit.

With plastic, tape, and fans, he'd set up a negative air pressure zone to carry the dust outside instead of letting it spread through the rest of the house. To ensure its effectiveness, he'd coached the homeowners and Alex on opening the door as little as possible, so when he heard the latch, he expected his employee.

Instead, Kerry stepped into the kitchen, and her mouth dropped open. With cabinet doors and appliances missing, the room did look like a gap-toothed kid. She and her husband, Fletch, were first-time homeowners, and Hale's youngest clients ever.

He lowered a couple more cabinet doors to the pile he'd amassed. "Can I help you?"

"I just wanted to see how it's going."

He summarized what he and Alex had done before lunch, then resumed breaking down cabinets, figuring if she had questions, she'd ask.

She turned a slow circle, studying the space. "I've changed my mind about the refrigerator."

Hale straightened away from his work, leaving one side of a cabinet tipped toward the floor, half unattached. "I put the order in for the cabinets weeks ago."

He'd visited Chimney Creek before moving to quote out

work for the Johanssons and several others. Kerry had insisted on being his first project, so he'd put in the orders for materials in advance of relocating.

"Yeah, but this is the fridge. I'm having one of those super-wide ones delivered." She waved an invoice and laid it on what was left of the counter. "It'll come before the kitchen is ready for it, but it'll keep."

He glanced at the paper just long enough to verify that it listed the make and model of the refrigerator. "If you change the size of the refrigerator, you have to change the cabinet measurements too. There isn't clearance for a super-wide in the original plan."

"The customer's always right." She forced a condescending smile.

Whoever had coined that phrase ought to be sentenced to a lifetime of dealing with unreasonable and very wrong customers. He moderated his tone. "To accommodate a larger fridge, we have to change our cabinet order. Since the cabinets were custom to begin with, a modification now will mean paying fees to adjust the plan. And the lead time is six to eight weeks, which could mean delaying installation for a couple of weeks. So it'll be more expensive and take longer."

Her mouth scrunched in frustration. "What happened to being on schedule and on budget?"

"The schedule and budget both rely on the customer's requests. If you change your requests, they change too."

She huffed and rolled her eyes. "Figures. Contractors are all alike."

He swallowed a flare of anger. "In this way, we are. But I'll be up front with you. I'll run the new numbers this afternoon and get you an adjusted quote so you can make an informed decision about if you want to move ahead."

"Of course I want to move ahead. I already ordered the fridge."

"I'll get you the update just the same." He'd have her sign

off on it too, since he wouldn't do the work and then have her claim he'd misled her.

The back door creaked again, and Alex stepped in. He sidestepped to avoid Kerry's exit and went to work removing the pile of debris, leaving Hale to his own work and thoughts.

Those thoughts were anything but peaceful as he now had two strained conversations to look forward to. One, with Kerry after he got a new quote on the cabinets. Two, with Morgan once he arrived home.

At the end of the workday, when he presented the new time frame and prices, Kerry's frustration showed on her face, but she and Fletch signed off on the changes. Maybe, after some more time to think about it, she'd realized she only had herself to blame.

Somewhat encouraged, he headed home to face Morgan. He half expected to find her on his porch, waiting, but the chairs there remained empty. He let Dax out and didn't spot her over the fence. He unpacked some more, made dinner, mowed. No Morgan.

Only after night fell did he spot a light on in her kitchen, evidence that, at some point, she'd come home.

What was she thinking in there? How long would it be until the situation blew up?

That night passed and then the weekend. He saw her dogs in the yard, but not her. They attended the same church, but she didn't cross the sanctuary to talk to him. When he took a step her way, thinking it might be best to get the conversation over with, she made a quick exit.

On Monday morning, they both headed to their detached garages at the same time. Kerry would throw a fit if he arrived late, but he waved to Morgan anyway. If she responded in a way that signaled a willingness to talk, he'd do it. But she didn't so much as glance in his direction.

six

· · ·

AFTER A DAY of removing old flooring from the Johannson's kitchen, Hale showered first thing on arriving home. As he pulled on a fresh T-shirt afterward, a knock at the front door sent Dax bolting to greet their first official visitor.

He'd expected Morgan for days, but somehow, the sight of her, with her red hair, milky skin, and blue eyes—sad and dull tonight—still hit him with the power of a fire hose. Talk about a blast from the past.

He clipped a lead to Dax's collar and pushed open the door. Though he held fast to keep Dax from jumping on her, she knelt to the dog's level and greeted him first.

Finally, she straightened. "Can we talk?"

He'd answered the door, hadn't he? "Sure."

She moved to the closest chair on the porch. Taking a seat in the other would mean brushing past her knees in the tight space, so he followed Dax down the four steps to the lawn.

Other than the loose strands of hair near her face, which swayed in the breeze, Morgan sat perfectly still, hands folded between her knees, focus fixed on him. Her irises held the same blue-gray as the distant mountains in the pictures Brady kept posting from his trip to the Rockies. Not a speck of joy or animation lit her features. "You recognized me right away?"

He nodded.

"Did you know before you moved in?"

He shook his head no.

"Why didn't you say something?"

He'd been wondering that himself. They hadn't started off on the right foot, but his silence had been more about her failure to recognize him. And yes, it was immature, but what kind of person left and missed the last few days they could've had with their best friend?

"I can't believe you'd move in and not say a word."

He sighed. She didn't seem to have come for a fight, and he shouldn't spin this that direction. "It's been twenty years. A lot's changed. I thought we could let the past go."

"Go? How?"

He lifted his shoulders and crossed his arms. They could shake hands, stick to their own yards, and pretend to be nothing more than neighbors, but the red splotches appearing on her cheeks suggested this wouldn't be that easy.

"You're the reason for everything." Her voice strained.

"What?"

"You know how my parents are. They loaded us all in the car a few days before your family moved and didn't tell us until we were hours from home that we were going to the cabin for a few days. They'd packed our bags in secret and everything. Mom swore we'd be back long before you left."

Hale huffed. "Yeah, like twelve or fourteen hours."

"She had the dates wrong. But as soon as I learned their plan, I started calling and messaging, but you didn't respond. When I went to your house the morning after we got back, your house was empty—and I know you were there the night before. I saw the cars. You left without even saying goodbye. You ghosted me."

"Not until after you did." He clamped his mouth shut.

Twenty-year-old pain wasn't supposed to feel so hot to the touch. He'd been through far worse than being betrayed by a thirteen-year-old friend.

"What does that mean?"

"Days before you left with your family, you were hardly around. My mom said sometimes people don't know how to say goodbye, so they cut ties early. I couldn't believe you'd do that, but then you all but avoided me and went on a trip."

"I called you as soon as my mom let me."

Neither of them had their own cell phones at that age, so she'd called his family's landline. He never heard the message itself, only his mom's summary of it. He'd gotten subsequent messages, but in those, she hadn't explained the surprise nature of the trip. Or at least, he didn't remember her doing so.

"You know how my parents are. No idea is too crazy, too spontaneous. Remember how scared I was they'd up and move us to Florida?"

When her grandparents relocated there, her mom made a comment about joining them because it was sunny and warm. He'd found Morgan crying by the creek over it, afraid of being uprooted. She'd said that was how her family did things—suddenly, with no warning or plan. That all it would take was a stray idea, and everything could change.

In the end, it was his own family that left, not on a whim, but because of his father's job after months of looking into options.

"They moved with about a month's notice when I was finishing eleventh grade, and it threatened all my plans—not only did I have friends, and I was a year from graduating, but Aunt Dorie had worked it out so I could get school credit for working for her, and she was helping me figure out and apply for college and scholarships. Thankfully, my parents let me stay here with her, and things got better for me after that. She was more structured, you know? But that trip just before you left was a nightmare. You were my best friend."

And she, his. They'd spent hours riding bikes, exploring fields, building a treehouse. They once got stuck up there until Morgan's parents called the police because they couldn't find her. They'd navigated the change to middle school and then high school together. And then came news of the move, and he'd written his Pre-Move Bucket List—a project he'd used to camouflage the one thing he really wanted to do: kiss her before he went.

After all, she'd had his heart for years, and he'd needed her to know it. He'd wanted to forge a connection that could survive the miles, and at thirteen, he'd banked on a kiss doing the trick.

"But then you bailed on me," she finished.

The memories turned bitter. He'd wanted to spend every waking moment with her, but after the kiss, she suddenly had a lot more chores she claimed she had to do. And then she up and left town. Apparently he couldn't blame her for that, but the truth remained. The same kiss that bound together all the loyalty and affection his thirteen-year-old heart could muster to her had sent her heart skittering in the opposite direction.

"We were bound to lose touch no matter what."

"It didn't have to happen like that."

He nodded and worked his jaw. "For what it's worth, I was hurt too."

"I couldn't control my parents. They're good people, they just . . ." She sighed heavily. "Mom swore up and down she thought your family wasn't moving until the following week. She apologized profusely that they'd cut it so close."

"What about before you left? And the night you got back? You could've seen me then."

"Before? I did see you."

"Not as much."

She shrugged and shook her head like she didn't know

what he meant. "As for when I got back, you weren't answering my calls. I knew you were angry, and I didn't think you wanted to talk to me."

"I saw the writing on the wall."

"Which was what?"

"That you didn't care as much as I did."

She tilted her head, her eyes tired and sad. "I cared so much. I went over in the morning, even though I knew you were mad at me. But you were already gone. I cried every day for weeks after that, and you can bet I don't do well with surprises anymore."

Dramatic much?

She must've read his skepticism on his face because she rose. "I drove my parents nuts, asking so many questions about what we were doing after that, determined not to be taken off guard again. Still, it was a shock when they decided to move." She huffed. "Anyway, without my plans and my focus, I never would've made it through vet school. So that impulsive getaway was a formative experience, but it didn't have to be such a painful one."

His abs tightened as if to deflect a gut punch. She was right, of course. They'd each made some decisions out of hurt that snowballed the situation. She'd taken a step back. He'd stopped responding. She hadn't come over. He'd left without a goodbye.

The first move had been hers, but he'd responded with harsh choices that blocked her attempts at reconciliation. If he'd faced the hard conversations, maybe they would've remained friends. He just hadn't seen many examples of that working, what with the way his parents never did find common ground. So instead, perhaps, he'd cut things off exactly like his mom had explained—to get it over with sooner than later. "You're right. I'm sorry."

She let out a shaky exhale. "So."

"Is this when we get reacquainted?" he asked.

She scratched her cheek and forced a smile. "You know my parents left and I moved in with Aunt Dorie. You know I went to vet school and started working in Chimney Creek. That pretty much sums up the last twenty years. What about you?"

"No relationships?" The question must've come from his teenage self, the one who'd orchestrated their kiss, because he no longer had a right to ask about her love life. And why did he want to?

Instead of telling him off like she could've, she simply shook her head. "Nothing serious. Relationships . . . Well, as someone who doesn't like surprises and changes in plans, I guess it only took a few dates to figure out I'd rather be on my own, focusing on the things that are most important."

The most important things weren't relationships? That told him all he needed to know about her.

She eyed him. "What about you?"

"I'd rather be on my own too. Not because relationships aren't important—they are. But because marriage doesn't usually work."

Her eyebrows flew higher. "You were married?"

"Engaged." He and Tanya had fought as much as his parents had during his childhood. But Morgan already thought poorly enough of him without him admitting he couldn't keep the peace in a relationship. "Didn't work out."

"Let me guess. You saw the writing on the wall."

He glared.

She flinched and dropped her gaze.

"So we're not going to be friends again," he said.

"Guess not." She focused a faraway look toward the street, almost like she could see them flying by on their bikes. "I don't know why I was so attached to you. I got in trouble for those times you talked me into swimming. And remember when you convinced Hannah to sled down the steep side of the sledding hill? She broke a bone."

A finger, but he didn't try to defend himself because he did feel guilty over that one. He'd pulled Hannah out of the snowbank, walked her home, apologizing the whole way, and brought her soup the following day—cans of it he bought from Hank's Convenience with his allowance, inspired by who knew what.

Morgan stepped closer to the edge of the porch. "All these years later, you're still the same, letting your dog run around on a leash that's a total joke, laughing it off when he eats my food, which could've caused life-threatening issues for him. Secretly infiltrating my life like it's some big joke to you."

"Yeah, all of this is so much fun. I'm having the time of my life." He tightened his grip on the leash. Though he'd never admit it, he'd almost forgotten he was holding it. Dax hadn't so much as tugged on the line, but he heard the dog's quiet panting from a couple of feet behind him.

In front of him, Morgan's chest rose and fell, as if she kept drawing air to lay on more guilt only to find words inadequate.

He knew that feeling well. It had prevented him from answering her messages after he'd moved away. What would the point have been? Their lives were headed in different directions. "I didn't reintroduce myself because we were just kids back then, and no history changes who we are now."

She crossed her arms, shoulders hunched. "Who?"

He climbed the stairs. "Strangers. Destined to stay that way."

She nodded once. Hints of relief softened the lines between her brows. "So you'll back off the committee."

"The committee?"

"The fundraising committee for the animal shelter. I'm on it."

He should've known she'd be involved with that too. "You might not have much faith in me, but that shelter needs all the help it can get, and I can be part of that. Dax was a life-changer for me. I believe in rescues, and whatever you think of me, Mili seems to like me, and I doubt your aunt will turn away my help." He pulled open his front door and jostled the line, silently signaling Dax to enter.

"My aunt isn't involved with the shelter anymore." By the strain in her voice, quite a conflict powered the rift that left the animals under Morgan's care and not her aunt's.

Hale unhooked Dax from the leash and closed the dog inside. When he turned back to Morgan, her frustration had morphed. Her brows slanted, and a deep frown cut her lips.

He stilled like he'd heard the click of a landmine. "What happened?"

"Aunt Dorie passed away three months ago."

An ache opened in his chest. He leaned his shoulder on the doorframe. Morgan adored her aunt, and that, more than anything he'd done, had shaped her. Her aunt's example was why she'd developed a love of animals, stayed in Chimney Creek, and gone into veterinary medicine.

Her frown trembled. Instead of looking to him for help or comfort as she once might have, she stared toward the front walk.

"I'm sorry." He'd meant his first apology, but this one came from so far down, his voice rasped. He hadn't lost family members he'd been especially close to, but he'd lost friends, and even years later, that still hurt sometimes. No wonder Morgan, just a few months after such a tremendous loss, hadn't been welcoming to the bothersome new neighbor. "You all right?"

She laughed ruefully. "Yeah, Hale. I'm having the time of my life."

And with that, she went back to her own place.

seven

. . .

THE FOLLOWING EVENING, Morgan raised her garage door and stood in the opening. Boxes and plastic bins from Aunt Dorie's storage shed filled a good portion of one of the parking spaces. Morgan had moved these, the last of her aunt's possessions, here to avoid paying rent on the storage space and so she could sort through the collection at her convenience. Since then, she'd spent most her time settling other matters of the estate and assuming full ownership of the veterinary clinic.

She'd been working out here the day Hale moved in. The bittersweet emotions of her task weakened her defenses, so no, she hadn't gone over to meet the new resident on move-in day. And now, knowing who he was and that he was right next door and that nothing was the same as it'd once been between them only added to her grief over people she'd lost so unexpectedly and so completely.

"He's right next door, but he might as well still be hundreds of miles away." She spoke to the boxes, but what she really wished was that Aunt Dorie was here to hear her.

She wasn't.

But God was.

She prayed—okay, more like complained—about her former friend. She'd gotten an apology, but not closure, perhaps because said apology had come with a fair amount of blame. Some of which, perhaps, she'd deserved.

The sweet, fresh scent of the breeze sifting the early summer leaves reminded her of how Hale had smelled like a mossy, wooded paradise yesterday as he'd stepped out of the house. Since they hadn't been especially close, she assumed he'd just cleaned up after work.

As if the fact that he smelled good mattered one way or the other.

She opened a blue plastic bin.

A quilt lay folded inside. She lifted it out, but couldn't guess the significance, if there was any. Before she donated an heirloom unawares, she snapped a picture and sent it to her parents, asking if they knew the quilt's story.

Their choice to move away all those years ago had wounded her, but over time, their relationship healed. They'd gone to support her mom's parents through a tough diagnosis, and she couldn't fault them for that. Plus, they'd allowed her to pursue her dream by living with Aunt Dorie, and though schedules weren't really her parents' thing, they'd remained steady in their weekly video calls to stay in touch, a tradition they maintained even now. That was more of a connection than lots of adults maintained with their parents.

Morgan opened the next box and found it brimming with old magazines. She wedged her hands under the cardboard to carry the collection to the recycling pile. As she lifted, pain grated through her lower back. Then more buzzed through her heart at the sound of footsteps and dog tags in the driveway.

Knowing who to expect, she turned, and sure enough, Hale edged around her car. Fresh off a run, his shirt stuck to his toned chest. The muscles in his arms and legs suggested he lifted weights instead of relying wholly on cardio for staying in shape. The happy way Dax tagged along, panting and tongue lolling, only added to the attraction.

To think, this man had been her first kiss.

And the first to break her heart—which was the part that mattered now.

"Here. Let me." He swept the box into his arms. "Where to?"

Her pride complained, but the discomfort in her back eased. She pointed to the recycling bin, then turned away when she caught herself admiring how the load brought out the definition in his shoulders.

The last of her anger washed into sadness. As kids, they hadn't known how a friendship could end badly, how they could hurt each other, how long that hurt would last. Now, thanks to each other, they did. That loss of innocence meant they could be nothing but uneasy neighbors. Strangers, as he'd said.

She opened another box, hoping he'd lose interest and leave. Beneath the flaps and yellowed newspaper, she found a serving platter. Cartoon birds with blue gingham handkerchiefs tied over their heads marched around the rim of the dish. She set it aside to investigate the other contents. If it was all the same dated pattern, she'd donate the box.

Dax's nails clicked on the concrete and his tags rattled, but she couldn't hear his owner. Maybe Edie and Eileen had a point about Hale's ability to move quietly.

She plunged her hands into the box and unburied a stack of matching plates. She fished around, feeling for smaller objects that may have been stacked in the surrounding space.

Hale's voice came quiet and low. "I can't believe she's gone."

Grief welled, and she swallowed to quell it. When would the simplest things stop sinking her emotions?

He lifted the platter silently, as though he'd gone to extra care not to scrape the ceramic against the concrete. "She used to keep this in her china cabinet."

Morgan hadn't remembered that.

He ran his fingers over the lip of the dish. Grief showed in the slant of his eyes, the single crease in his forehead.

He'd liked Aunt Dorie that much?

She tried to call his bluff. "You can have it, if you want."

He chuckled and returned the platter as carefully as he'd lifted it. "Geese have never been my thing."

Couldn't blame him for that.

"This must be hard for you." Gentle compassion carried his voice.

The concern seemed all the validation her sadness needed, because her eyes swam with moisture.

"How did she die?" His subdued tone persisted, reminding her of how she spoke to children who accompanied their parents to her office when a pet was unwell.

Except those kids could trust her. She couldn't trust Hale. Their past aside, he'd moved in next door and kept his identity a secret.

He stepped forward and looked into the box at the top of another pile, one stacked full of artwork. With a quiet swish, Dax's white face and fudge-sauce eyes appeared at her side. The dog licked her cheek, sparing her from having to catch a tear she'd failed to subdue.

Hale glanced from the framed pictures to Morgan, looking for an answer.

"Heart attack."

"It was sudden?"

The question hit like an arrow. After years of following plans so carefully, Morgan got sloppy. Crawford Fielding, one of Chimney Creek's most eligible bachelors, noticed her. She'd asked Aunt Dorie to cover the evening shift at the clinic so she could join him for dinner at Pie in the Sky, a pizza place that occupied the top half of a building downtown. During that shift, she'd died.

Morgan's presence wouldn't have changed the outcome, but she couldn't shake the guilt. She'd been off having fun while, elsewhere, tragedy struck. She hadn't looked at a man twice since. At least, not until one jumped her fence and turned out to be her long-lost childhood friend. But he, more than anyone, wasn't worth the risk that came with romance.

She braced her hands on the sides of the box. "Like you said, we're strangers." Her vocal cords ached with the strain of maintaining composure. "You're not supposed to ask personal questions."

Her sniffle must've taken the edge off her complaint, because he frowned at her sympathetically before he returned to studying the contents of the box. "These used to hang in the clinic. Are they worth anything? They look like originals."

The sudden switch from the woman she'd loved to the value of her possessions righted her unsteady emotions. She swept a hand over her face. "Aunt Dorie wasn't much of an art connoisseur."

"You should display them again." He pulled one out of the box and held it in both hands, taking in the details. Though he'd had the nerve to mention money, he hadn't lost the care-filled expression.

A pang shot through her, a desire to stand up, wrap her arms around him, lay her cheek against his shoulder, and allow his strength to hold her up. With that look, he didn't seem like the sort of man who'd refuse an old friend a much-needed hug.

But then what?

Besides, he'd just been running. A hug wouldn't be the pleasant comfort her imagination conjured.

She trained her focus on the painting. From this angle, she could make out a boy and a dog, but not much else. "Even

Aunt Dorie didn't keep it in the office anymore. She made the place over a while ago. They don't fit the look."

"Too bad." He returned the painting, and grit scraped beneath his sneaker as he stepped back.

Dax nudged her shoulder.

On reflex, she scratched the dog behind the ear. Maybe Dax would take a hug, but she didn't want to try it with Hale standing right there. She'd cuddle with Rose and Violet when she returned inside.

She stood, careful to assume a confident posture she knew would match Hale's even before she turned around and saw him standing there, just a foot and a half away. "You were right. I tried to connect with you, but not as hard as I could have. I'm sorry."

Half his mouth dipped into a frown, and he looked toward the street as if monitoring his exit strategy. "I shouldn't have asked for an apology. I know you were busy the night you got back."

Busy? Her family hadn't had anything special going on. She shook her head.

His shoulders shifted, as if his regrets weighed as much as that box of magazines. "I went by your house that night, stood out on the sidewalk."

"Why didn't you knock?"

"I saw you through the front window. You were at the table, eating with your family. Smiling. Happy." He shrugged. "I wasn't feeling it."

The desperation of a missed close call, like the time she'd missed the bus home from school, ached in her belly. "Maybe you were too far away to see it, but I hardly ate a thing that night."

He nodded a few times. "Look, we were kids. I've been meaning to let this go for twenty years now. So . . ." He lifted his open hands. "I'm sorry for your loss and for not saying goodbye like I should've."

"And for moving in next door to me without telling me."

"And for that. Although I didn't know you'd be my neighbor until Dax reintroduced us."

"When you were moving back, you could've looked me up." She maintained active profiles on two of the major social media sites. If he'd wanted to find her, he would've had an easy time of it. Speaking of, she could probably learn more about him and the life he'd lived these last twenty years on social media.

"Don't take this the wrong way, Morgan, but . . ." He shook his head. "I didn't come back looking for you. I enjoyed pedaling around the neighborhood with you as a kid, but childhood friends don't usually stay that way their whole lives. I figured we'd run into each other eventually, but I was hoping we could let bygones be bygones. Move on with our lives."

"You're right next door. You're on my committee."

"We can manage that, can't we?" He drew his focus to her face, studying her like he really wanted an answer.

She couldn't let him be the better adult. She nodded. "And again." Her throat tightened to prevent her next words, but she swallowed and forced them out. "I could've behaved differently too. I'm sorry."

"You're forgiven. I've had enough fighting. I'm here for a simpler life. For peace."

She caught herself squinting, trying to decode that one.

Instead of hanging around to explain, he led Dax away.

eight

. . .

MORGAN COMPENSATED for her hyperawareness of Hale at the fundraising committee meeting by ignoring him. She focused instead on the nine others who had convened in the library's meeting room to solidify plans for the shelter walk. Following Aunt Dorie's tried-and-true process for organizing all the details, the event coordination had flowed so easily, she'd almost called off this meeting.

"You all have really outdone yourselves. I think all that's left to do is divvy up the tasks we're responsible for during the event, unless someone ran into a snag." She paused to look around the table.

Committee members shook their heads.

Hale cleared his throat, low and purposeful, like the noise caused by a rumble strip. But whatever question he wanted to ask would likely be answered as the discussion continued.

If anyone would help her keep this meeting on track, her friend would, so she focused on Hannah. "You can set up the registration table, right? Make it look cute?"

"Sure." Hannah shot a glance at Hale.

Squelching the flair of betrayal, Morgan checked the notes on her tablet for the next responsibility.

"I have some ideas." Hale's declaration stilled the room, save for Eileen, who made a note on her legal pad. "Why do only a dog walk? We've got two months. That's plenty of time to add more dog-related events to draw more people. We could have spectators, in addition to participants."

His speech collected nods of agreement from most of the others. Even Hannah lifted her head until Morgan caught her eye and she sank back in her seat.

"More events?" Edie asked.

Another member nodded, confirming.

Eileen tapped her pen against her lips.

Hannah cringed and shrugged toward Morgan as if to say Hale's ideas might not be all bad.

"Spectators in Chimney Creek?" She struggled to hide her annoyance. "The dog-loving portion of the town already participates in the walk. They can't both participate and spectate."

"If we do multiple events, they can." Hale kept a steady gaze on her as if she, and not he, needed to be realistic. "Besides, to save the shelter, this needs to be bigger than the town. With social media, a few posters, and a press release, we can draw people from surrounding areas. Duluth, Superior, maybe even from as far east as Lakeshore—"

"Save the shelter?" She scoffed. He wasn't some kind of hero, and even if he were, they didn't need one. "This is the event we always do, and it's always been enough."

"But you need more this year." His focus settled on a red-faced Mili. "You *have* told them."

Mili rolled her lips in until no pink showed.

Morgan's equilibrium slanted, and her plans—Aunt Dorie's plans—rolled toward the rails. "Mili?"

"We need to raise more this year." She lifted her gaze, met Morgan's eyes, then reversed the process until she seemed entranced by a spot on the table.

"How much more?"

"Oh. Well. About ten times more."

"What?" Morgan's question, loud with shock, caused the shelter director to jump. "How? Why?"

"Building maintenance issues. An increase in the animals we've taken in. And we're in the red every single year. We're maxed out. Something needs to change."

"Or?" Morgan's breath stuck in her lungs, waiting.

"Or the shelter will close."

Morgan had been standing at the head of the table, but now she sank into her seat. They needed ten times their usual funds, and Mili had waited until the eight-week mark to tell everyone? Everyone but Hale Bastian?

"We can do it," he said. "I have a plan."

A plan? Him?

Nothing he dreamed up could rival the tried and true method they'd used for years. Yet he spoke with the confidence of the hero in a sports movie, swooping in with an unheard-of game plan to beat the fiercest opponent. "In addition to better, more widespread marketing, we need to add events."

Committee members leaned forward in their seats. Betsy, who owned the local bookstore, typed notes in her phone.

Hale leaned his arms on the table, looking broad and strong and capable as he scanned his roomful of supporters. Even Eileen met his gaze with a sort of businesslike respect.

How could Mili have kept this from her? If a new plan was necessary, everyone knew Morgan was the best person to come up with it. She just needed some notice.

Something Hale must've had, because he continued to pour out ideas. "We could set up an agility course and rent a pool for a jumping competition." He motioned to a couple of the business owners at the table. "We could rent tables to local vendors selling pet-related merchandise. Betsy, does your store sell any pet-related books? Jon, you could bake dog treats, in addition to normal bakery options."

Hale had been introduced to everyone on the committee before the meeting started, but he'd only indicated recognizing two people from his childhood—Hannah, who'd been Morgan's friend since kindergarten, and Jon, the baker, who'd been two years ahead of them in school. But of course the pretty bookseller's name had stuck with him.

Not that Morgan was jealous.

He continued. "We'll need a great big adoption tent to try to clear out some of the overcrowding."

Mili's eyes grew owl-like behind her glasses. "We could have a costume contest. And a best trick contest." Her volume, formerly quiet with embarrassment, grew with each suggestion.

"A stay contest?" Bernice, an office manager for the local mine, smiled. Morgan knew Bernice's dog well, and he had a decent shot at winning that contest.

Betsy lifted a slender hand and had the courtesy to look to Morgan—she alone seemed to remember who was in charge here. "I have a friend who's a photographer in Superior. She's an animal lover, so I bet she'd be willing to come help us for an afternoon. She could take some shots we could use for marketing. Plus, I've seen some cute photoshoot ideas that sound like they've been effective for increasing adoptions at other shelters."

"Wonderful," Hale said. "Check with her. See if she'd want to rent a booth too. She could take pet portraits."

"What you're talking about is a full day of events." Desperation had elbowed into Morgan's voice. She gulped, attempting to subdue it. She'd learned from her work with dogs that the key to dealing with an alpha male depended on remaining cool and collected.

"Maybe two. We can call it Dog Days of Chimney Creek." Hale swept his hands through the air, inviting everyone to imagine a banner.

"Ooh." Mili bounced in her seat. Actually bounced. "We

could do the contests and vendors on Saturday. On Sunday, we could have a pancake breakfast before church, then do the walk after. Adoptions running both days."

"We already reserved the park, so the date is set." Morgan's heart thumped fast. This was getting away from her, morphing into a completely new event. It was all too much, too quickly. If they overhauled everything without thinking it through, they would miss important details. "It's only two months away. You're talking about a massive event."

"Chimney Creek has to be the most generous community there is," Jon said. "If we come together, we can do this."

Hannah's eyes pleaded with her to understand. "It'd be worth the work to save the shelter, and I think Hale has a point. We're more likely to bring in that kind of money if Chimney Creek can pull in outside visitors."

"Sure, we have to save the shelter, but it's just not possible to change this plan. We don't have time."

Bernice raised her hand. "Think of all the families that would be positively impacted by the adoptions we could facilitate at a big event. Animals become a part of the family. They offer companionship, exercise, socialization. They teach kids about responsibility."

"And if they're in homes," Mili said, "they're not in an overcrowded shelter."

Morgan agreed. She really did. But . . . "We've only done the groundwork for the walk. There are so many details that go into these events." She lifted her hand toward Jon before she realized it was shaking. Quickly, she lowered it back to the table, but Hale was watching her closely.

Had he seen?

No matter. She needed to lead the committee. Hale could brainstorm all kinds of wild ideas, but realizing the plans the committee made fell to Morgan. They could not pull off an event the size he'd suggested in the time they had. When they tried and failed, they would be even further from saving the shelter than they were now.

"How much will we charge vendors?" she asked. "What will we provide for them? A tent? Tables? A promised amount of advertising? And what if we invest in those things and don't get the vendors? Or we do bring it all together, but Chimney Creek can only bring in so many visitors? Or it rains and no one comes? This is a huge risk."

The room quieted. Members exchanged glances.

"Some risks are worth taking," Hale said.

Jon scribbled some notes on a scrap of paper. "I can head up the vendor section. Make a plan, email it to everyone, then get it rolling."

"Is everyone willing to take on that much?" Morgan's fingers curled around the portfolio of the original plans. "Because if we do this, responsibilities will go from having one little part of the walk to having to organize something as large as the walk all on your own. We'd need a contest organizer. Someone to advertise. An adoption overseer to ensure the animals go to good homes. It might be better to simply inform people of the need and ask them to meet it instead of spending all our time putting on a show that may or may not result in raising ten times more funds. If it rains the day of—"

"Rain is a risk with the walk anyway," Hale countered.

That was what she got for mentioning the same concern twice, but she was flustered. "We've just . . . We've always . . ." She scanned the table for help. If only she'd known of the shelter's precarious position sooner.

Betsy lifted a few fingers. "I'll head up advertising."

"I'll work with Mili." Bernice smiled at the shelter director. "Together we can make sure the adoption portion goes smoothly."

And on down the line, one volunteer after another signed on to run another portion of the two-day extravaganza that would replace the simple dog walk. Hale had hijacked everything.

Did they even need her anymore? Maybe it was best that they didn't, because she worked from six thirty in the morning to seven thirty in the evening most weekdays. Her schedule had no give, especially not for an event of this size.

Hale's suggestions would dash her carefully laid plans, changing something that had once been dear to her and her aunt into an event that was both unrecognizable and impossible for her to contribute to in any significant way.

He was the newcomer, but thanks to him, she was now the odd one out.

———

Hale watched in horror as Morgan wiped beneath her eyes.

No surprise, she hated his ideas. Still, she once could rally to protect a good cause—especially one like the shelter—and he'd never had to tiptoe around her when they'd been kids. That was one of the reasons he'd liked her. Where had all her fight gone?

"I think we've doled out all the large responsibilities besides the dog walk itself." Hannah focused a gentle smile on Morgan. "I know the walk was always your aunt's thing, but I could oversee that portion so you could be the festival coordinator. With all these moving pieces, someone needs to be in charge."

Morgan shot Hale a murderous glare.

One he was beginning to understand. The shelter walk had been Dorie's project?

"Coordinating an entire weekend will take two people." Mili scooted closer to the table and pointed at Hannah. "You oversee the dog walk. They can act as co-presidents of the overall event." She flicked her finger back and forth between Hale and Morgan without even looking their way.

Was Mili that oblivious to the dynamics here?

"Mili—" Morgan started.

But then stopped. Who knew why.

Hale picked up the cause. "That won't work."

For the first time that day, Morgan nodded to agree with him. "With the clinic . . ." She scratched her temple with shaking fingers. "There's a lot on my plate right now, and adding all this . . ."

Was she about to step down entirely? A volley of guilt whistled by his ear. He hesitated, waiting for someone else to see the issue and offer a different solution.

Eileen tapped her pen against her mouth for about the fifth time. Edie stared at him. He wasn't sure how much of the conversation the woman heard, but she'd taken copious notes. If he got a look at her legal pad, he suspected they'd all be about him and not the event, since he seemed to be the only thing she focused on.

Morgan sniffed and continued. "I can let you guys do your thing, but I have too much . . . Um. I don't know how I could . . ."

More guilt shot through the conference room, a direct hit in the center of his chest.

"You're not stepping down." Mili's eyes had somehow grown even wider than normal.

Hannah blanched.

Morgan blinked rapidly. "I don't have time to act as coordinator for an event so large, but if you all think it's necessary, then I get it." She stared at the table and nodded like a child who'd agreed to donate her favorite doll to the less fortunate.

They may not be buddies anymore, but maybe he wished they were. Because he wanted to comfort her, make her smile, carry her burdens. He couldn't take away her role in an event her aunt had handed down to her.

"I'll act as your assistant." The offer came out weak. He cleared his throat and threw as much charm as he could into continuing. "Assign me as much as you need to. I'm good at taking orders."

At least, he had been at one time.

The sadness on Morgan's face edged toward skepticism.

He couldn't blame her for her doubts. She had an idea of how things should play out, and he didn't always agree. But as long as she was serving the larger event, he could comply with her plans, couldn't he? He offered a smile and prayed it didn't look tortured.

Hannah reached past Jon to lay her hand on Morgan's. "You worked with your aunt on this for years. You know more about running this than any of us. We need you, and we have a whole committee for a reason. Time to put us to work."

Edie read something on Eileen's paper, then declared, "This will be a real treat!"

Morgan's throat worked with a hard swallow.

She stared at her folder of plans a couple of beats too long, but when she turned her gaze back to the committee, she seemed stronger. More hopeful. "Okay. Let's do this."

Thank you, Lord. Maybe he hadn't just agreed to a task that would make his next two months a battle of wills.

Maybe.

Item by item, they discussed responsibilities and members volunteered for assignments. Several tasks didn't fall clearly to any one person's portion of the event, so Hale volunteered, taking on some general coordination duties without waiting for Morgan to tell him what to do.

"When you've written up your plan for your portion of the event, email it to me with your next steps and whatever tasks you need help on. And then I guess we'll . . ." Morgan glanced at Hale, ". . . take it from there."

She was as leery as he was. He reminded himself again that he believed in the shelter and needed it to exist. Also, he believed in not taking away one of Morgan's ties to Dorie.

Another look at her solidified his resolve. She lowered her gaze toward her papers, and her lashes dipped like they had the day he'd kissed her. Only the little smile that had rounded her cheeks then was replaced by the hollowness of stress and sadness.

———

When the meeting closed, Morgan watched Hale and Jon walk out together.

A throb of disappointment warned her that some part of her had been too attached to Hale's presence in the room—despite all the trouble he'd caused. Some part of her was apparently hoping he'd morph back into her best friend.

Hannah bade the other committee members goodbye as the room emptied. Morgan shoved her belongings back into her tote and checked the seal on her water bottle before settling it in an outer pocket. By the time she pulled the bag onto her shoulder, she and Hannah were alone.

Her friend donned a goofy grin. "I see why he's had you so flustered."

Morgan's fingers tightened around the strap of her tote. "Because he's ruining my life?"

Her expression turned sympathetic. "Not your life. Just the shelter walk as you knew it."

No, her life. He'd scarred her as a kid, he was a nuisance as a neighbor, and now he'd ambushed her in front of her committee.

"He doesn't know how things work here. He left when he was young, and he certainly doesn't know anything about what the shelter needs or what the town is capable of. We've never hosted an event so large, and now he wants to throw it together in two months?"

Hannah tucked her chair in. "It'll be a lot of work, but he

did say you could assign him as much as you want. You could have some fun with that."

"It won't be fun if it flops. It's all a big unknown. Will we break even?"

"God provides what we need. And around here, He often uses the people of Chimney Creek to do it."

Morgan ducked away from the table. Maybe she shouldn't be so attached to the way things had been. Maybe all of this would go as well as everyone thought.

Maybe.

Except hastily changed plans tended to bring unintended consequences.

She flipped off the conference room light. Hannah walked beside her up the stairs and through the foyer of the library. A round of laughter rose from a gathering of patrons. The sign indicating book club was in session explained.

"I know it's different than what she always did, but I think your aunt would've liked this."

"If she wanted the event bigger, don't you think she would've made it that way years ago? Why was the walk always enough in the past and now, suddenly, it's not?"

"If the shelter's budget has never been balanced, it was only a matter of time until it came to this." Hannah bumped her with a side hug. "And this new take on the event builds her legacy, don't you think?"

"The only thing it's building is Hale's already problematic ego."

Hannah chuckled and pushed open the door to the parking lot. "So, if anyone else had suggested the additions, you would've seen them in a more positive light? Like, if Mili or I had made them?"

Misery swirled. "Probably not."

Hannah tilted her head with a pitying smile. "It's going to be okay. Aunt Dorie would've liked this. I promise."

The statement rang a little too true. Aunt Dorie had been

the voice of reason twenty years ago, assuring her that her parents hadn't meant for her to miss Hale's departure and that he probably left the way he did because he couldn't bear to say goodbye. As Morgan grew more and more attached to the plans she made in the years that followed, Aunt Dorie encouraged her to remember that some things were out of her control and she had to let God be God.

She'd been working on it, but then God had taken Aunt Dorie home so unexpectedly, and all Morgan had left to go on were the plans they'd made together.

And still, unfortunately, Hannah was right. Aunt Dorie would've put the animals' well-being over Morgan's frustration with Hale and her preference to follow the original plan. If she really was committed to carrying on her aunt's legacy, that's exactly what she'd have to learn to do as well.

Lord, help me.

nine

. . .

HALE SCROLLED through the list of vendors Jon collected. In the two weeks since the meeting, the baker secured reservations for all the vendor booths they could accommodate at the Dog Days of Chimney Creek. The fees they paid ensured the whole affair would at least break even. On top of that, many vendors opted to contribute ten percent of their profits from the day to the cause.

But what are we missing, Lord?

This had been way too easy. He scanned the list again and saw it. If they drew the kind of crowds he hoped, those people would need a food option in addition to the bakery's offerings, yet none of the local restaurants had signed up.

For planning purposes, he'd scoped out the park where the event would occur. The preliminary map he'd drafted had filled the parking lot with vendor booths. A two-lane road also ran through the location. Initially, he'd thought some people might park there, but if they set up food trucks along the road, attendees could park on the surrounding streets. Besides, banning cars from the grounds would render the park safer for attendees.

Did Chimney Creek have any food trucks?

Hale's Internet search struck out.

He checked his watch. At five p.m. on a Saturday, Morgan might be home to ask.

Anticipation rushed him, and he anchored himself to the couch. He saw her almost daily over the fence, and he'd teased a couple of smiles out of her. So maybe their old connection wasn't completely dead.

Things hadn't been going as smoothly with his client, Kerry Johansson. He'd been walking on eggshells with the homeowner since they'd had to change the cabinet order to accommodate her new refrigerator. Then, yesterday—the day he'd planned to start installing the flooring—she announced she wanted five-inch-wide planks instead of three-inch.

Thankfully, a local store had the width in stock, but the wood needed to acclimate to the house for three days. He'd delivered the load to the Johanssons' before the weekend, but now he couldn't begin installation until Tuesday. A delay that had resulted in more complaints from his finicky homeowner.

Relationships of all kinds soured.

And when he marched over to Morgan's to talk her into adding food trucks to her carefully maintained plans, he'd only prove it again.

So, he should probably go do that straightaway, before he went on believing more and more that their relationship was different from all the rest.

He sighed. If only he hadn't made himself her assistant, they wouldn't talk so much, and he wouldn't be battling the resurrection of a crush he'd buried twenty years ago.

Why had he let her shaky hands and teary eyes get to him like that?

She wasn't his old friend anymore.

She was a gorgeous veterinarian with the power to override his common sense with a pair of puppy dog eyes.

Forget going over there. He texted Jon to ask if any food trucks operated locally.

While he had the phone out, he checked the time. Six thirty? That was long past Dax's dinner time. By now, the dog would usually station himself beside Hale's spot on the couch, drooling and begging for his evening allotment of kibble. Perhaps, in the new house, he'd found an extra comfy patch of sunshine somewhere.

"Dax?" He checked the dining room, but the windows didn't stream with sun this time of day. No Dax lounging on the hardwood around the table and chairs.

He hadn't gotten to hanging blinds in the guest room yet, so those windows did light up the room with sunny warmth, but still no Dax.

"Dax, dinner!"

No scuffle of paws. Concern swirled through his gut.

"Dax?" He scanned the kitchen as he passed, then took the stairs two at a time. "Hey, bud."

Still no response.

In his own room, he circled the bed. No dog beside or on top. Maybe under?

He dropped to look but saw nothing but gray carpeting.

Where else could he be?

He cringed. If Dax escaped and Morgan found him, Hale would never hear the end of it. The front door hadn't been open when he'd checked the dining room, but the side door was in a bit of an alcove he hadn't looked into. An alcove with carpeting, where Dax might even decide to curl up.

Hale checked the second-floor bathroom on his way to the stairs, then headed down. A glance assured him the dog also wasn't in the first-floor bathroom, so he continued to the alcove.

The door was shut. No dog.

"Dax?"

He peered down the stairs to the basement, but the door at the bottom remained closed.

Finally, one last place occurred to him.

Hale returned to the living room and bent to look into Dax's kennel.

There lay his goofy mutt, blinking at him.

"Don't you want dinner?"

The dog wagged his tail and reached a paw toward Hale.

"Well, come on, then."

He stepped away from the opening, but Dax only sighed and stilled his tail. Hale's heart sank.

"Hey, buddy, what's going on?" He felt nothing unusual as he ran his hands over the dog's thick, white fur, but Dax let out a sigh merged with a whine.

Hale had been less alarmed when he couldn't find the dog at all.

———

Morgan lifted the painting Hale had uncovered among Aunt Dorie's belongings. If any of the knowledge she'd gained in her high school electives remained, this had been done in oil. And she suspected Hale was correct that it was an original.

The piece featured two children standing beside a dining table. A black lab stood on the table, licking one of the kids' faces, while the other boy held a stethoscope to the dog's chest. In the background, a 1950s-looking mother had her hands to her face in horrified surprise that hadn't yet registered with the kids.

Morgan chuckled. Playing vet. How had the kids gotten a dog as heavy as themselves up on the table?

Oh, wait, one of the chairs was pushed back, and if she wasn't mistaken, there was a small pile of dog food on the table. The kids must've lured the dog to climb up. The artist had thought of everything.

Still smiling, she propped the frame against a box and reached for another. She liked these paintings, but Aunt Dorie had collected five or six of them. If they were worth something, she could sell most of them to benefit the shelter. Then, perhaps the event wouldn't need to be as large as it'd become.

"Morgan!"

She pivoted from the box. Whatever Hale wanted to fight about this time—

Wait. He was carrying Dax? Though his hold was secure, with one arm under Dax's chest and the other scooped around his bottom, Dax's legs dangled awkwardly. The dog peered at her as if pleading for rescue, resting his chin awkwardly against his own shoulder.

"What's going on?"

"I don't know. It's his dinnertime, but he didn't want to get up."

She met them in the driveway and had her hands on Dax even before Hale finished lowering the canine to the ground.

"He threw up his breakfast, but other than that, he was acting fine earlier. I guess he was a little sleepy when I put him out a couple of hours ago, but he wasn't like this."

The dog seemed groggy and, though able to keep himself upright, weak. He whined and hunched away when she touched his stomach.

"Does he often skip meals?"

"Never."

"Okay. It's impossible to say what's wrong here. You'd better get him to the emergency clinic."

"Emergency?" A note of increased concern rang in Hale's voice.

"He might have simply picked up some bacteria that's upsetting his stomach, but some other possibilities would require immediate care. There's a twenty-four-hour clinic forty-five minutes from here."

"That far? You can't help him?" His concern for Dax, so similar to what her own would be for one of her pets in his place, tugged at heartstrings she hadn't realized Hale Bastian could reach.

"In other circumstances, I could, but depending on what's wrong, he might need surgery, and my staff isn't on duty to assist. The emergency clinic is better equipped to give him the best care this time."

He rubbed his hand over his short hair, frowning. Dax sidestepped, as if to keep himself upright. Hale focused on her. "Come with us?"

Now he really had her heartstrings in the palm of his hand. "Sure. My car's closer. I'll get my keys."

She gave her dogs quick pats inside, then locked up and hurried back out.

In the driveway, Hale held out his hand. "I'll drive. You monitor the patient."

Though tempted to bristle at giving up control—she couldn't do much for Dax in the car—she did as requested. Mostly because he looked so deeply worried.

They coaxed Dax to the car, where Hale lifted the dog in. "Lord, help him. Please." He exhaled the prayer as he stepped back and shut the door, quietly enough that she doubted he meant for her to hear, let alone to respond.

Still, she appreciated the sign that his faith was more than just a Sunday morning habit. "God loves His creatures. He's the best vet there is."

He spared her a grateful smile as they crossed paths, her to the opposite side of the car to scoot into the backseat next to Dax, him to the driver's seat. As he followed GPS, Morgan settled back in the seat. Dax lay with his head resting against her leg, and she stroked the soft fur between his ears.

Outside the windows, her neighborhood gave way to small businesses as Hale turned onto Main Street. They navigated The Corners, the five-point intersection at the heart of downtown Chimney Creek, and eventually out of town and through the forested land between their small town and the larger ones to the northeast.

"Is this because of the chicken?" Hale asked.

"From my grill?" It'd been weeks since the little opportunist had stolen her dinner. "If that was going to be a problem, it would've manifested sooner."

Tendons flexed on the back of Hale's hand as he regripped the steering wheel. "I don't know of anything else he ate that he shouldn't have. That day was a fluke. He's usually a saint."

Judging by the behavior she'd seen from the dog on all other occasions, she couldn't argue. He seemed obedient and to have a good connection with his owner.

A good connection with Hale.

"Don't beat yourself up. We won't know anything for sure until they get a good look at him."

Hale rubbed his forehead but stayed silent.

She burrowed her fingers into Dax's lush fur. Dogs made good judges of character, and their behavior with their owners revealed a lot about the relationship between the two. Even during Chickengate, Dax had trusted and obeyed Hale. That meant Hale had proven himself trustworthy and dependable.

A trustworthy man who needed a distraction, and she knew just the one. "Have Edie and Eileen tailed you home yet?"

"What?" He glanced in the rearview mirror.

"They planned to once, but they claimed you snuck by them before they could follow."

"Snuck by . . ." He shook his head as if to clear a ridiculous notion. "Why did they want to follow me?"

"They think you're a secret agent. Something about the way you run."

He laughed once, loudly enough to prompt Dax to lift his head. "I run like a secret agent?"

"Technically, they said you run like an assassin from some movie, but because you help animals, you're probably one of the good guys."

He snorted. "Did you burst their bubble?"

She caught his gaze briefly in the rearview mirror. "How can I be sure you're not a secret agent? The whole contractor thing could be a cover."

He laughed once more, this time so quietly the sound registered like an exhale. "I'm no secret agent."

A mile passed in silence, and Morgan continued to stroke Dax's head. If only they had good options closer to home. But they didn't, so here she was, with a dog and a man she used to know.

Well, she'd known the boy version of him. The physical differences—the change from the gangly, grinning boy in her old photos into the handsome and fit man at the wheel—represented what must be much deeper changes too. He'd always been adventurous and intense. What experiences had those qualities led to, and how had those experiences shaped him?

Once upon a time, she could've asked. Now, she had to settle for so much less. "How do you think two people get to know each other again after so long? It's strange, knowing someone so well once and now, not."

"We could start with basics." He glanced in the mirror again. "How is your family?"

"Good. Mom and Dad are still up for anything. They took a seasonal job, running a rock shop outside one of the national parks out west. Courtney is married, two kids. She lives in Florida, near where they moved when I was a junior. James is a project manager in New York. He's pretty serious with his girlfriend, so we're all waiting for news from that quarter."

"James, huh?"

"It took him all three years of middle school to get people to stop calling him Jimmy." She smiled remembering how he used to scowl when someone got it wrong. "And your family?"

"Cam's a commercial pilot. Mom and Dad got divorced a couple of years after we moved. Dad's remarried and has two other kids. Mom says once was enough." He laughed ruefully.

"That must've been hard. Their divorce, watching them move on."

"Their fighting is also why I was always with you and your family instead of home with mine."

"I didn't realize." Uneasy sadness stirred her old memories.

Hale had been fun and always ready to jump through a loophole in the rules—and drag her along with. Come to think of it, though, those rules had always been set by her parents, not his, and without fail, her parents had been the ones to catch them.

The trouble had never been serious, but her parents would order her to stay in the yard for a few days and call his parents to report the concern. Hale would resurface the next day, no consequences or new rules to follow. Maybe they'd been glad to have him out of the house so they could focus on other problems.

He shrugged one shoulder, hand anchored to the wheel. "I didn't want you to know. You couldn't have done anything about it. Besides, kids go through worse."

Dax whined.

The rearview mirror showed Hale's brow furrowing.

Morgan shifted, wishing she'd managed to focus the conversation on lighter topics to give him a reprieve from negative emotions, but then, he was the one who'd started the questions about families.

He was also the one with all the secrets. If he hadn't told her about his parents as a child, and if he'd kept his very name a secret from her for almost two weeks as an adult, what else might he choose not to tell her?

———

"Some *emergency* center this is." Hale paced toward where Dax and Morgan waited in the large foyer of the twenty-four-hour clinic.

A technician—not an actual vet—had come out to check Dax's vitals on arrival. She'd declared him stable and left them to wait for the next available veterinarian.

Twenty minutes ago.

"Take a seat and relax." Morgan spoke the command softly and with a little smile, but she lifted one finger to point his attention to Dax.

The dog lay on the tile floor, head lifted and eyes fixed on Hale.

He hadn't considered his own stress would add to Dax's. He slumped into the seat.

Dax lowered his head, immediately more at ease.

Hale rubbed his forehead, his body already anxious to get up and move again. To do something. "You'd better distract me. You, um . . ." He struggled to switch his focus from Dax. "How long do you have to go to school to become a vet?"

"Usually about eight years. But, like I said, I had a plan. I took as many college credit classes as I could in high school and shaved a year off."

"And then you went right to work with your aunt?"

"Part of the plan. The only real surprise was losing Aunt Dorie and inheriting the practice so early on. But, otherwise, my life has mostly been studying and working. Pretty boring, but then I don't like surprises, so . . ."

"Surprises aren't all bad."

"Name one."

He'd moved in next door to her. But would she consider that as good as he did in this moment? He had little faith in this clinic, but having her here, knowledgeable and compassionate, relaxed him just enough that he wasn't breaking down doors to demand better service.

He glanced over, thinking of thanking her.

She arched an eyebrow, waiting for a response to her challenge to name a good surprise.

No need to get all mushy on her.

"My buddy Brady started an adventure travel company. I have to say, I'm surprised it's turned into such a success. He's a good guy, but not much of a businessman." He motioned toward Dax with his foot. "This guy was a surprise."

"How so?"

Hale ran his hand over his mouth. He might as well put his cards on the table, if she cared to look at them. "I met Dax during my second tour overseas."

"You served in the military?"

"With the Marines."

She studied him with interest and—was that respect? "What was that like?"

A broad question he didn't know how to answer. He focused on the part of the story relevant to the conversation. "There are a lot of stray dogs over there, and the culture is different. Dogs aren't treated the same. We found him scrounging for food and started taking care of him. He became a bright spot for us. I really think God brought us together for both Dax's sake and my own. I couldn't just leave him there. He wouldn't have had a good life, and I was finishing my contract, so it kind of made sense to adopt him."

"How'd you get him back? There has to be a lot of red tape."

"There are organizations that help service members bring home dogs they've bonded with. It's expensive, but we raised the money—more easily than I ever expected, a God thing, I'm sure—dealt with the requirements, and in the end, it was worth it. Whatever good I've done him, he's done me just as much."

Morgan gave him an appraising look, and he braced for her to ask about what he'd seen and done. He'd rather not give an extended explanation or draw her pity. Others had it far worse. He'd come home, he'd taken steps to readjust as best he could, and now he was out to enjoy a new, different chapter for both himself and Dax.

"He's tough," she said. "That'll serve him well."

He certainly hoped so. The dog was only about nine years old, and Hale was counting on several more years together. After everything he'd rescued the dog from, it'd be a tragedy to lose him now. Especially to something preventable, like stolen chicken drumsticks. "I am sorry he got over the fence that day."

"I don't think that caused this." She rubbed Hale's shoulder, and the touch warmed him like a ray of sunshine.

He ought to move away. This was Morgan, who was even more likely than others to launch his world into chaos. She'd already done it once, and after the relationships he'd had and seen succumb to jarring splits, he knew better.

On one level.

But, apparently, not all of his optimism had been crushed by his experiences, because he settled his arm around her shoulders.

The first signs of a smile brightened her eyes.

Despite where they sat and the circumstances that had brought them there, a sense of peace rose within him. God had provided Morgan to help him today, and everything would work out.

The grandness of that promise meant the feeling couldn't be trusted.

He closed his eyes and rested his head against the wall. If this was an ambush, he'd walk into it and worry about escaping later.

ten

. . .

MORGAN STEPPED THROUGH THE EXIT, which Hale held open for her, and into the night. The day's high of seventy-eight had mellowed so the temperature matched inside and out, though humidity made the outdoors clammy.

As Hale dropped his hand from the door, he brushed her arm.

Her body craved the warm weight of his arm around her shoulders again, his side next to hers, but maybe it was better that he focused ahead and tucked his hand into his pocket instead of reaching for her again.

She took a controlled breath. She should've left hours ago. But from the moment he'd carried Dax up her driveway, she'd been sucked in, and each passing moment left her a little more attached.

His claims that first day about Dax surviving worse than a stolen chicken dinner made a lot more sense now. A pair who'd met in a warzone would have a different perspective than her on what constituted cause for concern. Still, Hale had paid attention to his dog and had sought appropriate help as soon as an emergency arose.

He'd been agitated while waiting for Dax to be seen, but

once one of the vets had recommended surgery to remove an object from Dax's stomach, Hale had agreed with his old calm intensity. The only signs of his continued concern had been his declaration that he'd wait out the surgery in the waiting room, rather than returning home, and the way he'd rested his arm around her.

Now that the team had successfully removed the stuffed toy, Dax needed to stay overnight for observation. Hale scheduled an appointment to get the dog tomorrow and they were finally free to leave.

And none too soon. Morgan usually climbed into bed around this time, and perhaps her tired brain explained this inordinate amount of enjoyment she felt each time they touched.

They reached the parking lot.

"I don't know what's gotten into him lately." He passed her the car key and motioned her toward the driver's seat. Apparently, now that she didn't have Dax to monitor, he wouldn't continue to insist on driving.

She crossed to her door. "Moves can be stressful for dogs. You'll have to make sure he doesn't have access to his toys when you're not in the room."

His mouth tipped with begrudging agreement. He closed himself in next to her. "Is a little boring peace and quiet too much to ask?"

"Not in Chimney Creek."

"That's what I thought—until I moved back. Between Dax and Kerry Johansson, this hasn't been a cake walk."

She spared him a glance as she steered out of the parking lot. In the waiting room, he'd explained his troubles with the homeowner. "God looked out for Dax tonight. He'll look out for you too."

"I hope so." Hale sighed. "Anyway. Thanks for staying. You didn't have to."

When he signed off on the surgery, he'd told her he could

use a rideshare to get home, but she'd stayed. She could spare an evening for the sake of an old friend.

Especially when that old friend was also a military veteran with multiple tours under his belt. He'd served as a Marine. Infantry, she learned over the pizza they'd split in the waiting room. His reticence to share details, combined with his reference to needing Dax's help readjusting to civilian life, led her to believe he'd seen combat.

He was a hero with a soft spot for dogs.

She would not allow a hero with a soft spot for dogs to wait alone. "It would've cost a fortune to get a ride all the way back to Chimney Creek."

"Not as much as surgery. If that's how much operating on a dog costs, I'd hate to see the bill for a major operation on a human."

"Something to think about before you eat a stuffed parrot."

Hale chuckled, setting off bursts of joy in her own chest.

"Speaking of eating things . . ." he said.

She glanced from the road. After putting down more than half of the pizza they'd ordered, he couldn't be hungry again, could he?

"Jon sent the finalized list of vendors for Dog Days this afternoon. Did you see that?"

"I didn't see anything about food on there."

"Exactly. So far, only the bakery will sell anything to eat, and the crowd will need more than that." He tapped his fingers on his jeans-clad thigh. "I'm arranging for some food trucks to set up in the park."

"Food trucks? Where are you getting those?"

"There are a few in surrounding towns. Jon sent me a list of some he's tried."

"But we only have a few weeks to go. I'd rather focus on doing what we planned well and then raise the rest of the money through other efforts."

"What other efforts have a hope of bringing in as much as we need?"

"Those paintings, maybe. I'll contact the art gallery to help me figure out how much we might get for them. I'd like to keep one, but there are several."

"Unless they were done by someone famous, we'll still need everything we can get out of Dog Days. With food on site, people will stay longer. Plus, each truck will pay a fee to be there. And we could allow them to sell food but not beverages. If we sold our own drinks, we could funnel all the profits back into the shelter."

"That's pocket change."

"Pocket change adds up if the event's big enough."

If only she had the experience to know whether Dog Days would raise the funds they needed or not. What if they did all this extra work and the shelter still closed?

Well, she'd do her part. She'd get those paintings appraised and look for anything else in the last boxes that might be worth something. And she'd let Hale run with his ideas too.

"Do what you think is best," she said.

After all, he was a hero with a soft spot for dogs. He would only undertake projects he expected to help the shelter's bottom line.

He watched her quietly for about half a mile. "You don't like change."

"I said yes."

"But you didn't want to."

Morgan licked her lips, about to defend herself. But, well, Hale had a point. She *didn't* like change. Especially changes to plans.

"Sounds to me like a control issue."

"Hey, I haven't been trying to probe your psyche about this fiancée you once had."

Silence met the statement, giving her plenty of time to

wish she could retract it. But, as soon as he'd put his arm around her in the waiting room, questions had risen in her mind about his broken engagement. He was, after all, a hero with a soft spot for dogs. An *attractive* one at that. What had this other woman found fault with?

Because if Morgan was going to stick to her own plans for her life, she needed to know his faults.

"Interesting," he said, finally.

"What?" She fought to keep from cringing.

"You're jealous."

"I'm not." She inflated her lungs, hoping to muster belief in what she was about to say. "I'm not looking to date. Work is my priority. I don't have time for romance or anything that comes with it."

Even if she had enjoyed every second of having Hale's arm around her. Did allowing it—savoring it, even—make her a bad person when she had no intention of taking things further? Would he be angry now that he knew where she stood?

She glanced over.

Suspicion shaded his face. "But you have time to wait for hours with a man you haven't been close with in twenty years?"

Her mouth went dry. "A one-time outing like this is different. But when the clinic is open—which is most nights until seven—it's my responsibility to be there. And then I have my own pets to care for, my own life to manage. It's a lot, and honestly, I don't know how my aunt managed the practice on her own before I came along, but I guess now I really understand why she said a family wasn't in her plans."

"It wasn't?" A frown of disbelief shaped his voice. "She was always willing to spend time with us. Seems strange she didn't want kids."

Only because he didn't know her as well as Morgan did. She'd never known Aunt Dorie to date, nor to look into adoption or foster care. She had once commented on how much she enjoyed being an aunt, though. Which made sense. Being an aunt left more time and energy for a career than being a wife and a mom.

"So it all comes back to plans."

"Plans aren't all bad. God has plans too. Otherwise, He couldn't know the plans He has for us."

He snorted. "You're not really comparing your plans with God's plans, are you?"

"I'm just saying, if we're created in His image, planning makes sense."

"Planning to be too busy to have a life or tolerate the smallest surprises doesn't."

He just wasn't going to get this, and it didn't matter. She stopped arguing.

"You could hire another vet like your aunt hired you. Then you'd have more bandwidth."

Panic thumped in her chest. The last time she'd let someone fill in for her, it'd been Aunt Dorie, and it hadn't ended well.

"It's not that simple." She reached for reasons that didn't involve terror about history repeating itself, since she knew how unlikely that was. Theoretically. "My aunt hired me because she knew me. I can't trust Aunt Dorie's legacy to a stranger. Besides, it would still be my clinic. I'd still have to put in long hours to keep everything running smoothly."

"Because delegating is another thing you hate, in addition to change and surprises."

Morgan gripped the steering wheel with both hands and twisted them opposite directions. "I'm not against delegating. I delegated plenty at our last meeting. And I just delegated food trucks to you."

"Because I forced your hand. Just admit it. You have control issues."

"I'll do no such thing." Even if he was right. "Anyway, why do you care?"

"Besides you being a bear to work with?"

"A bear? Really?" She focused a death glare on the road.

Hale wiped his palms on his jeans. "It seems like this stuff leaves you unhappy. You were upset at the committee meeting when all the plans had to change. And maybe there's more to life than working. Maybe some plans would be better off changing. We believe God is bigger than we are." He paused, as if seeking agreement.

"Of course."

"If He's bigger, then His plans are too. That means He's going to surprise us, and our plans sometimes have to change. We can't see everything He sees when we try to predict what'll come next, but we can still trust Him."

If only it came easier, trusting a God who sometimes allowed tragedy. "Sometimes, the changes—the losses—are hard to acclimate to, you know? I did feel pretty secure once upon a time." She leveled a brief look at him. "Did you know how hard I prayed you wouldn't have to move? My parents like to say that everything has a way of working out, and between that and believing in prayer, I was certain you wouldn't have to move away, no matter what plans your family thought they'd follow through on. Maybe that's part of why I didn't try harder to reach you or to visit the moment we got home."

She checked on him again.

His eyes narrowed, but he kept his mouth shut.

Morgan refocused on the road. "I'd been praying and praying, and I was so sure God would give your dad a job in Chimney Creek. I really didn't think you'd end up going. But you did."

Even now, moisture collected in her eyes, sad for the tough lesson that hopeful girl had learned. Sad for her current self, who'd endured even worse. "Losing my aunt was another unwelcome change, but I thank God all the time that at least she and I made plans together, so I could pick up the pieces. And I think God's the one who put me on a path toward becoming a vet, and that plan has given my life purpose. Plans are in place for a reason. They can be real life-savers. So yes, changing the plans for Dog Days makes me uneasy."

"Except the plan for the walk wouldn't have saved the shelter."

"And I gave in. See? I'm not as stuck in my ways as you seem to think."

Hale shrugged.

She'd won. And to the victor went the spoils. "Now that I've answered all your nosy questions, I deserve to know about the fiancée."

Hale chuckled. "If I spill all my secrets, what'll Edie and Eileen have to keep them occupied all day?"

"I don't have to tell them."

"Nice try, Mo."

She hated that nickname, and he was the only person to ever dare use it on her more than once. Yet rather than annoyance, something calm and warm stirred in her chest. Reassurance, maybe? Because a nickname hinted at shared history. At longevity and permanence that were hard to come by. History meant she could relax, stop trying to protect or force things because all was secure.

Except this was Hale, who'd helped teach her that wasn't the case.

Now if only she could convince herself that falling for him wasn't part of the plan.

———

Hale owed Morgan, and he knew it. She'd dropped her project for the night, treated him and Dax kindly, and kept him company long past the time when Dax might have needed her expertise. Adding food trucks to the event hadn't upset her, and she'd also opened up to him. Morgan had extended an olive branch of friendship tonight. He'd be a fool to refuse it.

He could tell his story now, under the cover of darkness, while Morgan was half distracted by driving through the forest that surrounded Chimney Creek. That would keep things from getting too serious.

"When I graduated high school, I wanted to pave my own path, away from my parents. I thought I could show them how life was done—relationships and everything. There may have been some pride involved."

Morgan chuckled. "Who? You?"

"Hard to believe, I know. My parents both wanted me to go to college, but I enlisted as soon as I could. Before I left for basic training, I proposed to Tanya. We'd been together for two years and never fought the way my parents did. I thought we had what it took."

He trained his focus on the shadows edging the road, watching for wildlife. "At first, she seemed proud of having a Marine as a fiancé. We talked about getting married early on, but her parents convinced her to wait until she earned her college degree. I shipped out on my first tour when she was less than a year from graduating. Our plan was to get hitched when I got back, but by then, everything had fallen apart."

"What happened?"

He watched dark trees fly by. "I didn't want to worry her about everything happening over there. I bottled it up, but it came out in other ways. I got short with her. I wasn't great about keeping in touch. One day, I missed a call we'd planned. She emailed that she'd found someone else." The forest opened up for one house and then another. Ahead, the glow of Chimney Creek's streetlights announced the impending end of this trip and their conversation. "I've learned a lot since then. I'm not proud enough to think I know what it takes to make a relationship last anymore. The opposite, in fact."

"You're pretty committed to Dax."

The lighthearted suggestion was a gift. Or maybe she was just relieved he was as uninterested in a romance as she claimed to be?

"After my discharge, I worked for a contractor while earning my construction management degree. After a couple of years, I wanted to go into business for myself, but there was already a lot of competition in the area."

"There might not be a lot of competition in Chimney Creek, but I'm surprised there are enough jobs." Morgan dipped her head, as if judging the properties in the neighborhood that surrounded them. "New builds are pretty rare."

"I prefer remodels, anyway. The contrast between before and after. Making something old new again."

Was that what he and Morgan were doing? Renewing their old friendship? Already, the camaraderie bolstered him. What would this look like when they were done repairing the years of separation?

He'd kissed her once. A quick peck. If he got to kiss her again now—

Back up. No one would be kissing anyone.

What had they been talking about?

Remodels. The stability of his job. His reasons for moving here. "The people here are loyal. To their homes—they'll remodel over moving or building—and to a local contractor over the guy from the next town over. There's plenty of work."

She turned onto their street and, moments later, into her driveway. After she parked, he crossed behind the car and waited near the rear fender until she rose from the driver's seat. The house blocked the streetlight from reaching this far up her driveway, so they stood in navy shadows. She swept her fingers across her forehead and behind her ear, tucking away a stray lock of hair, probably.

He'd bet her hair was soft. Her skin warm.

"Thank you for your help tonight," he said.

Her nod was so slight, he could hardly discern it.

What had gotten into her? The same thing as him?

No, not Morgan who'd just told him she didn't want a relationship.

"Dax and I owe you." He ought to get going, but she just kept standing there. "Maybe a nicer dinner than one served on a paper plate."

That drew a smile, and he hated the shadows that kept him from seeing it better.

"It's been my pleasure. I enjoyed this." She chuckled, toyed with her hair again. "I mean, of course I would never wish harm on Dax. But this"—she motioned between herself and him—"this has been nice. It's been a long, long time, but I don't feel like you're a stranger anymore."

"Me neither." Gratitude propelled him forward. He opened his arms, and she stepped right into them.

For a moment, she rested in his embrace, resting her cheek against the hollow of his shoulder. When she stepped back, the cooler air of an early summer night swirled between them. Had he held her too long? Too close?

He'd get nowhere denying the truth. He was falling for her.

"I'll see you tomorrow." Gentle happiness softened her voice.

But they couldn't do this. Neither of them wanted a relationship, and that vulnerability—not to mention the thunderhead of attraction brewing in him—had relationship written all over it.

So instead of making promises of seeing her soon, he said, "Good night," and got out of there.

eleven

. . .

"SO, BAD NEWS." On the other end of the phone line, Mili paused dramatically.

Morgan finished signing off on a rabies vaccination record and passed the paper to Callie. That done, she stepped into her office. The preparation for Dog Days had been going far too smoothly over the last month, since Hale had hijacked her meeting and convinced the committee to shoot for the moon. Not that she resented him for it. Especially since their trip to the emergency vet with Dax two weeks ago.

A flutter in her stomach testified to a desire for more than friendship. Each time she saw him, she found herself musing about an alternate reality where they both had the time and inclination to indulge in a relationship and act on the chemistry that sizzled in the air between them.

Except, if the chemistry sizzled as loudly as she perceived, he probably wouldn't act as oblivious to it as he did. Which was just as well. Imagine. If they dated and broke up, he'd be right next door, glaring at her every time she let her dogs out. And since he had lingering scars over his last relationship and she had work to do, a breakup was the likely result.

Much better to skip the heartbreak.

"You're not going to guess?" Mili asked.

"I couldn't possibly." Mostly because her brain rerouted each train of thought directly to Hale.

"Samson is bleeding."

"Oh." Morgan's heart lurched. The dog might be afraid of most people, but he was a gentle giant. Had another dog picked on him? Or some other accident?

Did Hale know? Was he trying to comfort the dog even now?

"What happened?" She swiveled her desk chair to eye her own dogs, as if whatever had happened to Samson meant danger for them too. Both Violet and Rose snoozed peacefully on their fleece beds.

"Looks like he broke a nail, and the edge is really rough."

Relief allowed Morgan to exhale. A broken nail could be painful, but it was manageable—and not likely to have been caused by a fight.

"Okay. I'll swing by and get him cleaned up." She rotated her chair back toward her desk, where she pulled up the day's appointments. "What does your schedule look like today?"

"I can be flexible," Mili said. "It's Hale's schedule that'll matter."

"Hmm?"

If Mili noticed the high pitch, she didn't react. "Samson trusts him, and it'll take that plus a lot more muscle than I have to keep a dog Samson's size still while you take care of him."

"Good call." And so obvious a vet should've been the one to think of it.

Focus, Morgan.

All the animals in her care needed her to clear her mind.

"He comes every day on his lunch break," Mili continued. "If you come between noon and one, you should catch him."

"Perfect." She usually took her own lunch at about the

same time, so she didn't have appointments. "I'll see you soon."

She hung up and pushed away from her desk, drawing both of her dogs' attention. Even under the understanding focus of their sweet, brown eyes, Morgan couldn't justify her excitement at the prospect of seeing Hale. She'd seen him many times since their drive to the emergency clinic, and nothing of interest had happened. Today would be no different.

She had a job to do. He would help. It was as simple as that.

———

Hale parked at the animal shelter beside Eileen's car, but it was Morgan's vehicle beyond it that made him consider sneaking in the back way.

If he entered through the front, he'd have to pass the exam room. They'd see each other and have to at least greet one another. They'd probably get to talking. If their trip to the vet was any indication, he'd enjoy it too much. Even now, longing swirled through him.

He'd told her about Tanya, but apparently, he was forgetting some of the details of his own story. Like the painful lesson he'd learned from that relationship. He didn't want to battle his way through another heartache. He didn't want what his parents had had.

So, he'd been keeping his distance from Morgan. Not enough to make her feel snubbed—he hoped—but enough to keep them from indulging in fantasies that wouldn't play out nicely in reality.

He started around the side of the building. In the middle of the day like this, the side door should be unlocked as other staff and volunteers took dogs in and out. The added bonus to entering this way was how confusing Edie and Eileen would find it when he appeared from the back. He chuckled as he followed the cracked sidewalk to the metal door. He grabbed the knob, but it didn't turn.

Figured.

Something moved beyond the narrow window in the door.

None other than Morgan stood by the kennels, and she'd spotted him.

Some secret agent he was.

She pushed open the door and gave a friendly smile, as if it were the most natural thing for him to have come to the little-used entrance. "We were hoping you'd show up."

We. Not *I.* And though welcoming, her expression didn't give any indication that his presence meant anything extra special to her.

As disappointment pooled in his gut, his jaw pulsed with frustration. They weren't even in a relationship, and already, she was interfering with his peace of mind. "What'd you need me for?"

She led the way down the row of kennels. "Samson broke a nail in the yard earlier, and we want to clean up the jagged edges before he catches them on something and makes it worse."

The mostly black dog lay curled in the back of his kennel, licking his paw with his giant, pink tongue. Blood smeared the floor at intervals to match Samson's gait. When he spotted his audience, he lifted his head and thumped his tail.

"That's for you." Morgan chuckled. "He hasn't wagged his tail for any of the rest of us."

"Probably because he knows you want to get at that paw." Hale would lose trust with the dog for helping, but it had to be done. He lifted the latch and stepped inside the kennel. Once he'd closed it behind himself again, he squatted and extended a treat.

Samson eyed something behind Hale, and a soft rustle

indicated Morgan stepping farther down the aisle, giving them space. The dog rose to his tan feet and slurped the treat from Hale's palm. He dipped his head to see the nail in question. Still oozing and jagged and broken higher up than he'd hoped.

"We'll need more treats." He extended his empty hand. The dog sniffed it, then allowed him to pet his shoulder.

"Okay. I'll get my clippers too." Morgan's sneakers padded away.

He coaxed Samson into lying down. The animal resisted turning onto his side, but if allowed to keep his legs beneath him, Hale would never keep him down long enough for Morgan to do her job.

When she returned, she passed him the treats, then touched the dog's muscular shoulder. "Hey, sweetheart. Do you think you can let me help you?"

Hale thought about making a quip about Samson not liking the pet name, but the opposite appeared true. That or he was scared stiff. Either way, he went still.

Hale kept a firm hold. With a dog this size and in pain, Morgan's safety depended on him not losing control.

She offered the dog a treat, but Samson didn't go for it.

"Poor guy." She positioned herself by the injured paw, ran her hand down that leg, and held the foot fast when Samson tried to yank it away.

Hale struggled to keep him down, but a few seconds later, Morgan set down the clippers and dabbed powder onto the end of the broken nail.

She released the dog, popped to her feet, and stepped back. "All set."

His respect for her skyrocketed. Done already?

Samson bolted to the back of the kennel. There, the dog shook himself as if to shed all evidence of human touch and looked back and forth between his opponents.

"Sorry, sweetie." Morgan used her foot to nudge the treat in Samson's direction.

It bumped against his paw. Samson sniffed it, but instead of eating, he studied them. Probably best to give him space.

He motioned her to step out.

She cast a look back as she returned to the aisle, but instead of focusing on the patient, her gaze found him. "I feel like I hardly see you."

He had lost track of how many times he'd made Dax wait an extra ten minutes before going outside so she and her dogs wouldn't be out at the same time. But he smiled like their failure to cross paths was coincidental. "Miss me?"

She chuckled. "I've been wondering how Dax is."

"Back to one hundred percent, except the spot where they shaved his fur hasn't grown back yet." Now a few steps from Samson's kennel, he thought he heard the crunch of a treat, but when he turned his head to verify, he realized instead Morgan stood close enough that their shoulders nearly touched.

A hint of flowers swirled on the air. In the dingy tan of the shelter, her red hair and blue irises seemed to shine as she peered back toward their patient.

"Thank you again for your help." His voice came out gritty. He cleared his throat. "With Dax. And you were amazing with Samson just now."

She scrunched her nose, but instead of picking on him for getting sentimental on her, she pointed to their patient. "He's relaxing already."

The treat no longer lay on the floor. Samson circled in his bed and flopped down.

"Do you think he'll be ready for adoption by Dog Days?"

Adoption? Somewhere along the line, he'd decided to bring the dog home himself. Would've by now, in fact, if not for Dax's recent behavior. Introducing another dog while Dax remained unpredictable would only multiply potential problems, inviting chaos into the house.

Show me the way to green pastures, Lord. For all of us.

For now, that way didn't involve assuming ownership of the stray, as much as he wanted to. "By Dog Days, he'll be as ready as he can be."

For now, Samson had done well and deserved a break. They continued down the row.

"Do you know if Betsy got all the Dog Days posters distributed?" Morgan asked.

"To every pet supply store in fifty miles, and the social media shares have been good." He stopped at the rack of leashes. Since Samson ought to have some downtime, he'd walk one of the others. "A couple of papers are running our press release too. How about your to-do list? Need help with anything?"

"Amazingly, no. The tent company agreed to set up on Thursday so we can arrange the adoption area on Friday. That's probably my biggest concern now. Everything's planned, but it'll be tight, making it all a reality. We have to set up kennels. The beverage area. Signs and cones and agility equipment for the events. All within about twenty-four hours."

"We can do it."

"I drafted an order of events I'll email out soon." Morgan leaned against the corner that would take her to the exam room or the office. "The lady who runs the art gallery helped me look into selling those paintings."

"Oh. Yeah?"

"The artist lived in the state. She helped me figure out which gallery sold his art during his lifetime, and we called there. They'd be happy to display it for us to sell and think we could get around a thousand per piece."

Hale let out a low whistle. "Dorie was more into art than we thought."

"They say she would've paid less than that, but the artist passed away, and the gallery still has people inquiring about his work. Even so, they warned it takes a while for paintings to sell. I'll deliver them to the gallery, and we'll see what happens. It just might not be the quick moneymaker I'd hoped."

"So you don't get to cancel Dog Days."

"I guess not." Playful annoyance narrowed her eyes, and she bit her lower lip.

The memory of kissing her all those years ago ambushed him, and he turned to grab a couple of leashes. "Then I'll see you at Monday's meeting."

"Before then, I hope, neighbor."

Not if he could help it. But saying as much would hurt her feelings, and even if he didn't want to date her, he didn't want to hurt her. Actually, not dating her was supposed to keep them both from hurting each other any more than they already had.

"I guess we'll see, neighbor."

Smirking, she headed to the exam room.

Okay, so yes, his response had been delayed and awkward. But at least he hadn't made any promises.

He chose the three most energetic of the dogs, clipped them to leashes, and led them up front. Edie and Eileen sat behind the desk.

At the sight of him, Eileen bumped Edie's arm. "When did you get here?"

"Few minutes ago." He waved and held the door for the dogs.

"Does he walk through walls now?" Edie's question, inadvertently shouted, ended just as the door finished closing, so he didn't get the benefit of hearing Eileen's response.

———

As usual, Morgan's busy week kept her from social media, but on Friday night, as she relaxed into the weekend, she opened one of her apps. A block of text from Kerry Johansson topped her feed, quite a few negative reactions amassed beneath. Skimming yielded that the rant centered around her remodel.

She glanced toward Hale's house. They'd waved to each other a minute ago, as he went inside with Dax and she came out to her patio with Violet and Rose. But once again, the last couple of weeks had passed like the few before it. He'd worked with her as needed, like when Samson had broken his nail, but none of their conversations had touched on topics of any importance.

She was beginning to suspect he was avoiding her on purpose. So much for being friends.

Morgan clicked to see the full post, expecting that a vendor had failed to deliver on time, or perhaps the previous homeowner had boarded over a serious problem. Instead, Kerry ranted that Hale lied about time frames, kept raising prices, and disappeared for days when he should be working. None of this could be true. Did he know about this post?

With a flick of her finger, she navigated to the comments. Chimney Creek residents had left a whole string of responses, thanking her for warning them. At least five promised to cancel jobs they'd hired him for.

She tapped the icon to leave a comment of her own, defending Hale, but before she acted like she knew what was going on, she ought to learn the facts. Besides, he needed to know about this as soon as possible so he could mitigate the damage.

Indignation insisted she take the straightest route to his house, so she sat on the fence and swung her legs over, more smoothly than last time. When she pressed the doorbell at his side entrance, Dax let out two barks from inside, and then Hale appeared behind his screen door.

"Are you connected online with Kerry Johansson?"

His eyebrows pulled low, and he stepped around Dax and outside. "I'm not. Why?"

She passed him the phone.

A scowl deepened across his face as he read. "This is ridiculous. I have never had a client change so many significant things and have so little grasp on how that affects the entire process. Each time I got as far as I could until new materials she wanted arrived, I told her the exact days I'd be fitting in jobs for other customers. This was yesterday?" He scrolled up. "Yeah. Yesterday, she announced she wants to change the backsplash to this ugly shade of green the local stores have the good sense not to carry. I guarantee she'll regret it in a year, but it's her kitchen, so I ordered it for her." He moved his finger back down. "And she's . . ." He scoffed and shook his head. "She's costing me work."

He handed the phone back, mouth tight.

"What are you going to do?" Morgan asked.

"Give her a call, I guess." He brushed a hand over his hair. "Tomorrow, when I'm calmer."

She looked at the post again. "I've seen glimpses that made me think Kerry was a bit high maintenance, but I never suspected she'd be so unreasonable. Maybe I can get her to rethink this." She tapped to start drafting a comment.

He touched her wrist. "Don't get in the middle of it. I don't want to turn this into a war with people taking sides."

"But it already is. Except no one's on your side." She glued her focus to the screen, since that, and not the chemical reaction he'd started by touching her, was her reason for being here. "Oh, wait. There's a comment from Mili."

He stepped closer to read over her shoulder, and the air held hints of his woodsy scent.

Hale Bastian has been a godsend at the shelter. A reliable man of his word. There's got to be more to this story.

Not far below it, she spotted another comment.

He did some work for us with no problems. Sorry you're going through all this!

Not exactly a glowing recommendation. Certainly not enough to undo all the damage Kerry had done.

"What was I thinking?" He spoke quietly, as if to himself, but he stood so close, his breath registered on her ear.

"Thinking when?" She might comment on Kerry's post later, when she wouldn't have to do so in front of him, but for now, she tucked the phone into her back pocket and turned. She found herself standing almost toe-to-toe with him.

He studied her without stepping back. "Moving here."

"I'm sure you've faced more intimidating enemies than one ornery homeowner."

He let out a wry chuckle and looked away.

"Lots of people are glad you're here. Don't let Kerry get to you."

He sighed. If only standing so close could give her an idea of what he was thinking. She laid her hand on his shoulder, hoping to draw his attention back. For the sake of her ability to think, however, she should've kept her hands to herself, because the firm warmth of muscle under his T-shirt sleeve derailed her train of thought.

"I'm not sure Chimney Creek has what I came for." He moved his arm to shrug her off, so she lowered her hand. Only, his fingers caught hers on the way down and held.

His calloused hand clasped her gently, despite the anger and disappointment that had to be blazing behind his calm exterior. He was a warrior, but he'd told her he'd come for peace. Peace he must've felt here in his childhood, or he wouldn't have returned expecting to find it. She liked to think she was part of those positive memories. Reminding him of one might restore his sense of hope.

"You kissed me once," she said. "Remember that?"

Shock wiped his expression clear, and her gut twisted

with embarrassment. She'd meant to bring up a good moment, but that should never have been the one to slip out.

"I remember." His eyebrows twitched closer. "Why?"

A sheepish chuckle escaped. "I was just trying to remind you of better times." She loosened her grip on him, but he didn't let her go.

The corners of his mouth tipped up, and his gaze skimmed her lips. "And that was the best you could think of?" Was that a hint of smolder in his blue eyes? No? Just her brain playing tricks on her?

Embarrassment flushed her cheeks. "I thought you might think so."

His hearty laugh warmed the air between them. "You didn't?"

Why, oh why had she brought this up?

Desperate to downplay it, she met his gaze with a playful grin. "The kiss was disappointing."

Hale flattened his palm against his chest as if to cover a wound, but he laughed. Loudly.

Encouraged, she continued. "A little sloppy, if I'm honest. I hope you've improved your technique since then."

"Improved my technique." He repeated her words slowly, both challenge and humor underscoring his tone.

She'd been too cavalier. She ought to step back, reestablish distance, and—for the sake of her career and all her plans for her life—stop more or less challenging him to kiss her.

Except . . . She loved her job, but as she basked in the center of Hale's attention, her common sense melted into a puddle of anticipation.

He shifted closer, and the last dregs of her reservations lifted her hand to stay him. Or that was the idea, but instead of motioning him to stop, her palm smoothed over his shoulder, welcoming instead of rebuffing him.

"Morgan." Had his voice always held this much gravel?

"I've been thinking. If I have to go, there's something I think I need to do first."

She knew these words. This was exactly what he'd said to her the day he'd asked—

"Can I kiss you?"

At age thirteen, she'd answered with a very prim *yes, you may.*

In response, he'd scrawled her name on his bucket list and hadn't called in the debt until weeks later. Judging by the intent in his eyes now, he didn't plan to wait that long if she agreed, and somehow, at thirty-three, she possessed far less composure than she'd commanded as a young teen. She linked her hands behind his neck, and his arms fit around her waist. All she had to do was repeat her line.

"Yes." In her effort to get her voice working, she spoke too loudly. She dropped to a whisper. "You may."

He leaned in, so that as she finished, her lips brushed his. He paused there, their breaths mingling. This close, she could see the flecks of cerulean that gave depth to his pale blue irises. Then his eyes sank closed, and overcome by the rush of anticipation, her own followed suit.

Their lips met. As unhurried as the kiss was, it amounted to just one moment in a relationship that stretched so far into her past, she could also imagine it reaching years into the future. This was the kind of kiss a thirteen-year-old couldn't give or receive. In fact, she hadn't experienced it in her other forays into dating either. This connection had roots and wings and steady arms to hold her so she hardly needed her own feet. His lips shifted in a momentary smile, and the feeling of weightlessness multiplied as he kissed her again.

When the connection broke, she reopened her eyes slowly. He tipped his forehead against hers, exhaled, and finally loosened his hold on her. Balancing took all her focus. She wanted to pull him in again. She craved the impossible, the feeling of being secure in the unknown, where she could forget the plan and let her heart call the shots.

But what would this mean? For her? For her career?

And for Hale, who'd said he didn't want a relationship either?

The doubts anchored her to the concrete, preventing her from stepping closer again. Her arms grew so heavy, they slipped from his shoulders.

"How's my technique?" His voice held a gentle tease. His hands still rested on her hips, and his thumb slid up and down over her shirt near her waistline.

She had to blink and take two breaths. Finally, she laughed, rubbed her fingers across her cheek, and stepped out of his reach to where she could think more clearly. "Much improved."

His smile might've seemed smug, if not for the searching way his eyes roamed her face.

She motioned toward her yard, where the dogs played. "I should get back."

His smile persisted, as if amused he'd left her flustered. "Good night, Morgan."

"Good night." She'd never make it over the fence in this state, so she pushed her hands into her jeans pockets and rounded the front of her house.

Once she'd escaped his view, she stopped in the shadows of her driveway.

She had a legacy to carry on. Plans to enact. A shelter to save.

If even Aunt Dorie hadn't attempted to balance romance with her responsibilities, who was Morgan to think she could manage it?

twelve

. . .

INSTEAD OF GOING STRAIGHT to the Johansson's kitchen via the back door on Monday, Hale approached the front and rang the bell.

As planned, he'd called Kerry on Saturday, but she hadn't answered or returned the call. He'd half doubted she would answer the door, but moments after he hit the doorbell, Kerry Johannson stood in front of him.

She'd dressed for the day in jeans and a sleeveless sweater, and, for him alone he suspected, topped the look off with an expression of smug challenge. She knew exactly what prompted his visit, and she wasn't any sorrier for her actions than he was for his.

He prayed that this would somehow go better than he expected. "What you posted doesn't reflect the reality of what happened."

She crossed her arms. "If that's how you feel about it, I'll find a different contractor."

Wow. He'd considered that may come of this conversation, but he hadn't expected it to be the first thing out of her mouth. Then again, could he fault her for being as direct as he was?

"Another contractor will have the same problems meeting your demands—"

She scoffed and rolled her eyes. "I doubt that. This has obviously run its course."

Fine. He didn't need clients who bashed him publicly for delays and price increases caused by their own whims. "I'll clear out now and send you an invoice."

"An invoice? We already made that huge down payment. At this point, you owe us."

"The changes you made to your orders ate up the deposit, which I outlined for you in the updated invoices. You owe on the labor we've completed."

"Send it." She laughed humorlessly. "I'll forward it straight to our lawyer."

"Do that." He headed around back to clear his things out before he lost his cool.

He'd kept her informed every step of the way. She knew the cost of the remodel and each line item that contributed. A lawyer would tell her to pay the debt.

He hoped.

He also hoped she would listen, because once he reached home with a suddenly open schedule, he called other clients to move up their projects. The first three withdrew their projects. The next two weren't ready to start. By the time that changed, he suspected Kerry's opinion of him would reach them, and they'd back out too.

That would leave him without work. And without an income, he couldn't stay.

He should've seen this coming. Instead, he'd let himself focus on Morgan. The pain surrounding the last time he'd moved away had finally settled, and now here he was, on the verge of having to stir it all up again. Her life was here. His might not be.

But if he had to go, there was someone he wanted to bring with him if at all possible: Samson.

He stretched his rib cage with a deep breath and blew it out. "Come on, Dax."

Maybe the dogs would be fast friends, and Samson would be part of the solution, not a factor that made Dax's recent behavior worse.

Unfortunately, the shelter proved the wrong place to go to avoid Morgan. Her car sat near the door. She was probably attending to vaccinations and other needs. At least here, he couldn't act on any notions about repeating Friday night.

Inside, Mili worked the front desk.

Eileen's shout ricocheted from the medical room. "I've heard videos are the way to popularity right now."

"What?" Morgan, too, spoke loudly.

Edie must be with them.

"Online," Eileen said. "People love to watch videos. We should make one for Dog Days." Good for Eileen, keeping up with the trends.

"Oh." Morgan sounded dubious, and of course she did. Videos weren't part of the plan. "Okay." She paused, and he imagined her gulping down worry. "We can talk about it at tonight's meeting. There's not much time left, but maybe it'll make a good final push."

A valiant attempt to not let her fears win the day.

Mili leaned over the reception desk to get eyes on Dax. "Who do we have here?"

He introduced his dog. "Can you bring Samson out to the exercise area so they can meet?" The distance from all the barking ought to provide a calmer environment that would give the two the best chance at getting along.

"Sure thing. I'll get him now."

Nerves cinched Hale's gut. He'd formed quite a bond with Samson. If the dogs couldn't get along, he'd be forced to let Samson go to someone else. And a dog who looked like a purebred was sure to go as soon as the shelter listed him.

With another less-than-effective deep breath, he walked Dax out to the fenced-in area.

As soon as Mili led Samson out, he tugged toward Hale. Dax, playing fetch with a ball they'd found in the enclosure, didn't notice the Rottweiler until a return trip. Dax froze, ball in his mouth.

As Mili secured the gate, Samson tugged the leash from her and trotted to Hale. Not to be left out, Dax sprinted their direction. Samson rounded on him and growled, stopping Dax in his tracks as Hale grabbed the larger dog's leash. Alert, Dax dropped the ball and inched closer. Samson bared his teeth.

Dax cocked his head but thankfully had the sense to hang back until Mili hustled up and looped her hand through the end of the lead trailing from his collar. "Samson's guarding you," she said.

"I'd rather he didn't."

Dax took advantage of the slack in his leash to step closer. Samson lunged for him, and Hale braced himself to hold the line against the aggression and the corresponding tug of defeat.

Once he and Mili pulled the dogs farther apart and Samson settled, Hale caught sight of Morgan standing at the side door of the shelter, hand raised to shield her eyes as she watched.

"Let's try walking them around in here," Mili suggested. "Stay at least fifteen feet away. We'll see if they get used to each other."

If only he could cut his losses and leave before he had to manage a tricky interaction with Morgan too, but letting the dogs end on a bad note wouldn't set them up for future success. He and the director each led their charges in rambling circles as Morgan approached the fence. He tightened his hold on the leash and turned a corner, walking Samson a little closer to Mili and Dax. Dax still seemed confused about why he had to obey someone other than his master, while Samson kept a wary eye on his newfound nemesis.

Now just inside the enclosure, Morgan lifted her phone. Was she recording them? Given the snatch of conversation he'd heard inside, this must be for a promotional video for Dog Days. He didn't spoil the footage by asking. After all, he may never be able to adopt Samson. He couldn't protest including the dog in a video that could find him a home.

How he wished everything were different. Falling into place instead of falling apart.

As it was, his experiences said he wouldn't get the dog, let alone the girl.

———

If Morgan had to guess, Hale had decided as firmly as she had that they had no future together. Why else would he have avoided eye contact for the entire Dog Days meeting tonight?

She ought to be relieved he was so resigned to not distract her from the work, but part of her wished the decision hadn't been so easy for him. Because, despite her commitment to her career, her cheeks flushed yet again at the thought of that kiss.

She tipped her head toward her tablet screen to hide a foolish grin. This was not a move a committee chair with a career to consider should have to employ. As Aunt Dorie had once said, romance wasn't in the plan for her. She pressed her lips into a firm line.

"I can check with the high school." Hale's forehead furrowed as he typed on his phone. "They might be willing to lend us stopwatches."

That point settled, the committee looked to her for the next point on the agenda.

She glanced over all the notes she'd taken today. "I have to say, everyone, you're doing a great job. I'm impressed by how this is coming together."

With only three and a half weeks until the event, they had twice as many signed up for the dog walk as normal. Morgan didn't recognize about half of the names, which meant their marketing had spread word beyond the Chimney Creek regulars. Registrations for the stay contest, the best trick competition, and the agility course continued to trickle in.

"The last item on the list is Eileen's suggestion to use a video to spread the word on social media. It does seem like an effective strategy, so I took some footage of Samson and Hale, but I don't think we can just post it as is and expect it to do well. People like stories, though, and there are lots of those involving the shelter. If any of you are comfortable with doing a short video testimonial about how adopting your pet has positively impacted your life, we can incorporate that into a post to promote Dog Days and adopting in general. Any takers?"

Committee members shifted. Camera shy, perhaps?

She focused on Hale. "You wouldn't mind doing another video, would you? People would love hearing how you rescued Dax from a war zone."

His focus rose as if she'd startled him from a deep sleep. He blinked a few times, gulped, opened his mouth, then let it close. Maybe he didn't really understand her vision.

"We could do a little series," she continued. "Heroes and their dogs. Mili, have any police officers or firefighters adopted from the shelter?"

But Mili was staring at Hale, not paying attention to Morgan. The woman's eyes seemed to fill the entire circle of her glasses. "A war zone?"

Oh, no. Had Hale told her about his service and Dax in confidence?

"I was a Marine." His focus leveled on Edie and Eileen,

who gaped at him. He might've volunteered the fact only to prevent wilder stories from growing.

Morgan licked her lips and struggled for a strategy to turn the attention away from him again. "Whatever else we do, I think some members of the committee should speak too. I'll do one about one of my cats. Eileen, you should, too."

"I would if I had a pet," Betsy volunteered. "As soon as I get my own place, my first act will be to adopt. But, in the meantime, if you take a video, send it to me. I do social media for the bookstore, so I can edit it and add the information about the event. Just keep it short. Maybe twenty or thirty seconds. Unless, you know, you have a really special story." She lifted her eyebrows at Hale.

He avoided eye contact.

Morgan fumbled through wrapping up. As the group moved toward the exit, Hannah looked like she wanted to hang around and ask questions, but after a glance at Hale, her friend left.

He kept his place at the table until they were alone.

She held her tote in front of herself, handles in two clenched fists. "I'm really sorry. I didn't know that was a secret. Aren't you . . . You should be proud to have served."

"I'm not a fan of painting myself as a hero."

"Why?"

"We were doing our jobs." He trained his focus on her, softer, less shocked and frustrated than he'd appeared earlier. "I didn't enlist to have anyone make a fuss about me."

"Well, yeah, but . . . ." She let her argument peter off. "I'm sorry I spoke out of turn. I wish I could undo it."

A faint smile appeared at the corner of his mouth. "I very much doubt the possibility of that."

True. Edie didn't have a very wide social circle, but Eileen did, and she liked to talk.

"I'm really sorry. Is there any way I can make it up to you?"

"Not necessary." He pushed his chair back from the conference table.

Together, they made their way out of the room and up from the basement of the library to the first floor. Over a hundred years ago, the building had been a bank. Now, the wooden shelves of books and cozy corners furnished with comfy chairs, rugs, and lamps made even the marble floor and high ceilings inviting.

Hale's voice rumbled beside her. "With my reputation around town right now, using me in a video might do the event more harm than good."

"Actually, I was thinking the opposite." She spotted Ella, a librarian with a sunny disposition to match her blond hair, behind the circulation desk and waved before they exited to the front steps, awash in golden late-day sun. "Once people know your story, they might be less inclined to listen to unfounded criticism. Sharing a glimpse of your past might reverse the tide."

"You think so?" His voice held a new lift, but his eyebrows slanted with concern.

They arrived at her car. "It certainly wouldn't hurt."

"I'll think about it." He studied her for an extra beat. A beat most others wouldn't have taken. But instead of decoding the stretched moment for her, his mouth tightened into a polite smile, and he opened her car door for her. "Good night."

She tried to convey another apology for oversharing in her answering smile as she took the cue and got behind the wheel. He shut her in without signaling whether he'd received the unspoken message.

Rather than be caught staring after him as he headed for his truck, she headed home and tried not to let her curiosity glue her to her windows, watching for him to pull in next door.

thirteen

. . .

MORGAN PLAYED her favorite of the Dog Days promotional videos one more time—the last time, she promised herself. Although, did a promise mean much after how many times she'd already made and broken it?

On her screen, in a blue polo that amplified the color of his eyes and fitted smoothly over his confident posture, Hale looked every bit the hero he was. His retelling sounded more even and rehearsed than when he'd related the events to her, but the added snapshots of him and Dax together in the Middle East would pull on the most calloused heartstrings.

Meanwhile, Dax sat beside him on screen, showing his love of life and Hale with every wag of his tail. The video had somehow gotten a quarter of a million hits in the week since it'd gone live. Such a large number dwarfed her own six views.

Okay, maybe nine.

Still.

Based on the comments, many of the viewers planned to support the shelter or organizations like the one that had helped Hale bring Dax home.

She bit the corner of her mouth. Would it really be so bad to play it again? Unless perhaps, seeing him in person was an option . . .

Outside her dining room window stood Hale's house. Dog Days was coming up that weekend, but that didn't offer much consolation. They'd be too busy working to connect.

But then, the kind of connection she kept wanting was impossible. And he must've felt the same, or he wouldn't have made himself so scarce, despite still being painfully underemployed, thanks to Kerry.

Morgan had come home for dinner tonight, even though her work schedule was, as usual, packed, because she'd forgotten the chipotle ranch dressing for her salad. She could've used the French dressing in the break room fridge, but then there would've been no chance of running into her neighbor. Unfortunately, no matter how many times she glanced out the window, she saw no movement next door.

Viv Fielding had brought her cat in for a routine exam this morning. She said she'd asked Hale for a quote on finishing her attic, so he might be there. And that, of course, would be far better in the long run than him being home for her to accidentally-on-purpose encounter him.

Morgan pulled her focus from the window to take her last bite of salad. She didn't have time to track her neighbor. Already, she'd dawdled so much that she risked arriving late for her next appointment, which would throw off her schedule for the rest of the evening.

She dropped off her plate and fork in the kitchen. As she grabbed her purse, her line of sight strayed to the window again.

Finally, she was rewarded with a glimpse of—

Who was that?

The man in Hale's yard had his hair in a blond bun. He moved along the side of the house, gripped one of the windowsills, and lifted himself to see in. The guy was fit, she'd give him that, but this was not normal.

Heart racing, she called Hale.

The man dropped from the windowsill and skulked toward the back of the house. He wore jeans and a purple T-shirt. Not the sort of outfit she imagined on a burglar, but his brow furrowed as he checked his surroundings before disappearing around the corner.

Hale's voicemail picked up.

"There's a man at your house, looking in the windows. Are you expecting someone? Because he looks kind of . . . Well, at the risk of sounding like Edie and Eileen, he's acting kind of suspicious."

She hung up, jogged to a different window, and angled to see the back of Hale's house. Impossible from inside. She eased out the back door and snagged a glimpse of the man's boot disappearing into Hale's home through an open window.

With a gasp, she flattened herself against her house, then bolted inside. She must act quickly. Poor Dax was in there with that stranger. How would the dog react to the threat?

The benefit of small-town living was, she knew a couple of the local police officers. She dialed Christian Grant, whose dogs she treated and who attended her church.

"Hey, Morgan. What's—"

"I think someone just broke into Hale's house." The men had likely met at church, since Hale had been attending too. "The one where the Jacobsons used to live."

"You're sure?"

"A man climbed in through the back window. Hale isn't there, so I'm pretty sure."

"I'm on my way. But, Morgan?"

"Yeah?"

"Always call 911 in emergencies."

Her rapidly beating heart tripped. "I just don't know if that's what this is."

"Morgan." Christian's voice held a stern warning.

"All right." She bit her lip until it hurt and watched for any sign of the guy next door leaving so she could call this whole thing off. But she saw no movement. "Want me to call them now?"

"I'll call it in. Sit tight. If he comes your way—"

Her throat cinched with panic at the mere suggestion. "I'll call 911. Immediately."

"See you soon." Christian disconnected.

Within minutes, two police cruisers parked on the street. Christian and James, a rookie who'd grown up in Chimney Creek, approached the house. Too nervous to watch, Morgan sat in her living room, clutching her phone.

When it buzzed in her hands, she nearly screamed. After a glance at the display, she answered. "Hale—"

"I'm not expecting anyone. Did he leave?"

At least she hadn't called the police on an invited guest. "He climbed in through a window. I called the police. They're over there now." She went to the front to check their progress.

Both Christian and James stood on the front porch. The intruder had opened the door for them, as if he were right at home. Would a thief do that? It'd take guts, but that didn't make it impossible. "He's—"

Dax bolted past the intruder, across the porch, and onto the lawn. He assessed the surprised trio of men before sprinting down the sidewalk.

"He let Dax out." She couldn't risk the dog running out in front of a car or getting lost. "I'll get him."

Without giving Hale the chance to reply, she hung up and ran out.

———

When Hale parked in front of his house, Brady Lang stood on the porch like he owned the place. The two officers appeared less than convinced. Only the blond one looked toward the noise of Hale's car door. The one with dark hair—Chris, maybe? Curtis? They'd met at church, but the parade of people blurred in his mind—kept his focus locked on their suspect.

"Hey!" Brady grinned a greeting.

If looks could kill, the officers would have to arrest Hale for murdering his friend. Still, he couldn't have Brady charged with breaking and entering. He joined the group, showed his ID, and explained Brady was a friend before he scanned the street. "Morgan and Dax?"

"Thata way." Brady pointed to the right. "Sorry about that. He was chill until the knock at the door. I closed him in the office, but I must not've shut the door all the way."

No one occupied the sidewalk in the direction Brady had indicated. Hale looked to his truck, deciding whether to drive or proceed on foot, and that's when he saw Morgan round the corner from the opposite direction of the one Brady had pointed. She bent at an odd angle, hobbling as Dax gave her a rough go of it.

Hale jogged to meet her. As he drew close, Dax threw his seventy pounds into pulling toward him, and Morgan teetered.

"You all right?" Hale grabbed the collar, inadvertently overlapping his fingers with hers. Her skin was warm and smooth as she slipped her hand away. Heat that had nothing to do with the sunny summer day flushed him.

"I'm okay." Her chest rose and fell with panted breaths, and a sweet pink shaded her cheeks. And no wonder. If she'd circled the block since they'd gotten off the phone, they'd run at a good clip. Her attention flitted beyond him. "And your house?"

"An unexpected friend." On his front lawn, Brady and the

officers peered their way. Chris or Cody or whatever his name was, waved. Brady followed suit.

"I'm sorry about all of this," Hale said.

"He is deceptively fast." She pressed her hand to her chest, still winded.

"I should've said to stay inside." Not only had Dax put her through her paces, the home intruder could've been dangerous. "You didn't need to chase him down."

"I couldn't have him running out into traffic. Although he followed the sidewalk weirdly well for a loose dog." She drew a particularly deep breath and exhaled. "So false alarm?"

"Sort of. He did break in. You want to . . ." He swallowed the rest of the offer to introduce her to Brady. Connecting the two seemed like a bad idea.

Whatever ending Morgan guessed he'd wanted to say, she shook her head. "I'm late getting back to work." She checked her watch, then set off for her house at a hurried clip. "Really late." She flailed a hand—an afterthought of a wave—and disappeared inside.

Hale led Dax home. The younger cop left, and Morgan pulled out of her drive as Hale deposited the dog inside.

That done, he turned to Brady and shook his head. "You couldn't have called?"

Brady grinned, brown eyes swimming with trouble. "Who's the neighbor?"

"You'd know if you'd bothered to help her."

"I couldn't just run away." Brady motioned to the officer. "How would that have looked?"

The officer's name tag read C. Grant. No help with the first name. Whatever his name, he chuckled. "Unless you'd like to press charges, I'll be on my way."

He crossed his arms. "We'll settle this between ourselves."

Officer Grant's line of sight tracked back and forth between him and Brady. "Through legal means, I trust."

Brady guffawed and slapped Hale's shoulder.

Officer Grant's eyes squinted in amusement, but still he waited for Hale to nod his agreement before he left.

Brady grinned and wiggled his eyebrows. "Long time no see."

He scoffed, and they headed for the house.

Brady had the nerve to step ahead and get the door. "Why so grumpy?"

At the door, Dax rushed to greet Hale, and he bent to look the dog over more closely than he'd been able to outside. He'd healed completely from his surgery and seemed no worse for wear after his run.

He straightened and crossed his arms again. "I finally have a customer looking for a price quote, but I had to run out of there to deal with this. You upset Morgan. Two officers had to respond to the call. What about this should make me happy?"

With another trademark grin, Brady lifted his hands away from his sides, presenting himself as the bright side.

Hale continued to the kitchen, Dax and Brady on his heels. Sure enough, one of the windows remained open. He slid it shut and locked it.

"Since when are you so uptight?" Brady leaned against the doorframe.

Apparently he wasn't uptight enough, or he wouldn't have left a window unlocked. He checked the others. "The police were here."

His friend moved from his path. "Yeah, but no one got arrested."

Hale verified that the side door had also been secured, though he suspected Brady would've tried that before a window. Sure enough, the deadbolt remained in place.

"What are you doing?" Brady asked, following him to the dining room.

"I have to go wrap up the price quote."

"Okay. But you don't have to lock the place down. I'll be here."

Hale shot him a glare, then moved on to check the next set of windows. "Next time I lock a door, I want to know it'll keep people out."

Brady snorted.

"Shouldn't you be in Antarctica or something?"

"I'm between trips, remember? Antarctica's a great idea, though."

Hale verified the last room's windows, then knelt to check on Dax one more time. The dog covered his face in kisses.

"I thought commitment wasn't really your thing." An uncharacteristic edge of suspicion lowered Brady's voice.

A baiting statement like that didn't deserve a response. He did commitment just fine, or he wouldn't have excelled in the military. He had a house, a dog, and volunteer work. And, if he could get anyone to hire him, his own business. He held the front door open, watching to prevent another escape.

Brady sauntered onto the porch. "The neighbor's why you won't come work for me, isn't she? You've lived here for weeks but haven't mentioned her."

He pulled the door shut tight. "I won't work for you because you're the kind of guy who can't show up without causing a public disturbance."

"And you haven't mentioned the neighbor because . . .?" Brady's footsteps thumped along behind him across the porch. When he didn't fill in the blank, Brady took the liberty. "Because you know once I heard, I'd remind you of what happened last time you fell for a beautiful woman."

He paused at his driver's door long enough to glare at his friend, who stood with his hands braced on the porch railing. Lifting his voice to answer would only give anyone in earshot more to gossip about later.

He could only imagine what Edie and Eileen would do with this event once they heard of it, and that was without

Brady giving them reason to think Hale was falling for anyone. "I'll be home in an hour."

Brady groaned dramatically and slouched onto a patio chair. No doubt, he planned to go back inside as soon as Hale left. Joke was on him, since Hale had just locked him out.

fourteen

. . .

"I FEEL like I have to make an appointment to see you these days."

Morgan swiveled from her paperwork toward the door of her office.

Hannah entered, greeted Violet and Rose, then settled in the wooden chair next to Morgan's desk. "That'd be awkward, what with me not having a pet." Hannah shot her a significant look. "Would Dorie like you working this much?"

"It's what she did before I joined the staff here." She finished the note she'd been making and set her pen aside. "It makes sense I'd have to do the same now that I'm the only vet. Anyway, it seems I still have time for the occasional adventure." She related the story of the intruder and Dax's escape. "I'm glad it turned out to be nothing, since Hale and Dax have been through so much already."

Instead of laughing and agreeing the way she'd expected, Hannah tapped a nail on the desk, then lifted it to point. "You like him, don't you?"

"Hale?" She laughed and hoped the sting on her cheeks didn't mean a visible blush. "Romance isn't in the plan for me."

Hannah laughed. "Whose plan?"

"Mine. He lives right next door. Can you imagine sharing a property line with your ex? Because that's what we'd be doing if we dated and it didn't work out. Which it wouldn't, because I can't manage a relationship right now. Keeping up with all of Aunt Dorie's work is hard enough."

"The loss is still fresh, I'm sure." Hannah's face turned from sympathetic to hopeful in a moment. "But eventually . . ."

Somehow, Morgan had thought of Aunt Dorie and the clinic without thinking of the loss. At Hannah's mention of it, emotion swelled. She shook her head to diffuse the cloud. "There is no eventually. I've had to work hard to get everything I planned for, and I'll have to stick with the plan to keep it. As you noticed, I'm already having a hard enough time maintaining my friendships. To have more with Hale, I'd have to sacrifice my work, and I'm not doing that."

"Sure. Of course." Hannah changed the subject, but her agreement had been too easy. She didn't believe in the impracticalities of a relationship between them, and Morgan couldn't circle back and try to convince her again.

Not when, deep down, she was becoming less and less convinced herself.

———

Hale finished up with the price quote for Viv and Mark Fielding, a son and daughter-in-law of the couple who owned Hank's Convenience downtown. Basically Chimney Creek royalty, their good opinion might open other doors for him. Then again, level-headed customers like that might want to stay as far from drama as possible.

When he returned home, he found Brady where he'd left him, scrolling his phone on the porch. He didn't give Hale the satisfaction of complaining about being locked out, but they both knew who'd won that round.

Hale unlocked the door. "Let's head to the animal shelter and run with some of the dogs. They can always use more time out of their kennels."

Brady tucked his phone away and shrugged. "You're the boss."

So, half an hour later, they took two dogs each down the shelter's gravel drive toward the road.

"I usually circle this block." Hale motioned to indicate the shelter's property and the block it sat on. One mile per side, the run would provide more than enough time to learn his friend's purpose here.

Mili had said she would be heading out soon, but she'd entrusted Hale with a key. When she'd proclaimed it high time he had one, anyway, Brady had lifted an eyebrow at him. Now, he fell into step beside Hale.

An adrenaline junkie, Brady stayed fit to tackle any activity Hale could've thrown at him, and this run would prove no challenge, even though neither the Australian sheepdog nor the German shepherd—both mixes, of course—Brady had were leash trained. They immediately crossed paths, getting tangled.

Brady opened his arms wide, tugging the dogs until one ran on each side. "So why're you here?"

Hale checked, but his friend's expression was serious. "That's my line."

"I came to find out why you're here. So, let's hear it. The compelling reason you've turned down a chance to explore the best the world has to offer."

The young beagle Hale was supposed to control zigzagged in front of him, and he nearly tripped. He shortened the leash. Meanwhile, the lab mix in his other hand trotted along with them like a dream. "You came to recruit me?"

"I wasn't going to be that direct. Figured you'd see the error in your ways when you were forced to explain them to someone who can see for himself what you do and don't have going here." They turned from the drive onto the broad shoulder of the quiet country road, the dogs fanning out around them. "Scenery's fine if you like farmland, forests, and hills, I guess, but the world has more to offer."

"There's a state park nearby, and we have a lot of water too. Lake Superior. The Saint Louis River—"

"And you've got a key to the animal shelter. Livin' large."

He let his gaze wander the gentle swells of the land. Crops—potatoes, he thought, on one side of the road, corn on the other—swayed in the breeze, and the cry of a redwing blackbird rose like an echo of his childhood summers. "It's home."

This was the place of hope, imagination, and possibility. The place with pockets of peace, which he'd found nowhere else.

"Your family isn't here."

"But some of my favorite memories are."

"You're still supposed to be making memories."

"Who says I'm not?"

Brady pressed his hand to his chest in a false show of emotion. Thankfully, the sheepdog put an end to it by yanking on his lead and forcing him to hang on. "I will always fondly remember running through cornfields with you."

"What I don't get is why you're happy with all the responsibility of running a company."

"I set my own schedule, hire people for the parts of the job I don't like, and rack up crazy frequent flyer miles. I can go wherever I want between tours. Tell me that doesn't sound like the dream."

"Maybe for you. For all your employees, it's probably just a job."

"Is that what you're afraid of? That I'd treat you like an employee?"

A car approached, and Hale pushed ahead. Brady fell in behind him, all the dogs in the grass along the shoulder.

Once the vehicle had passed, Brady caught back up. "I don't want to hire you."

Hale scoffed. That's all Brady had tried to do every time they'd spoken over the last few months. Although it'd take a lot more than one job to justify turning Brady down again.

"I want you to buy in as a partner with equal say."

The beagle zipped off course again and nearly tugged the leash from Hale's fingers. He renewed his grip. "Partner?"

"Yeah. Of course. I don't want someone to boss around. I want someone who brings fresh perspective and can help maintain momentum. I can be a bit . . . impulsive. I've got a great team, but I can only be so frank with them, and vice versa. I'm the boss, after all. I need someone I can trust, whether it's with fresh ideas or with a group of tourists in the wilderness. Not many people fit that bill."

This whole time, he'd thought Brady was offering him so much less. "I'll think about it."

Brady herded the German shepherd away from the center of the road. "If you come on board and want to bring your wife along on some of the trips, that'd be all right." He cringed, belying the statement. "I mean, if you're really set on settling down."

Hale's feet, suddenly leaden, ground to a halt. "What wife?"

"Any wife." Brady continued, his stride easy.

Hale forced himself back into motion.

"Right now, the neighbor's looking like the leading candidate, but I've only been here a few hours." Brady cast him a sideways glance. "You got your eye on someone else?"

"I don't have my eye on anyone."

"So you won't mind if I ask her out."

Air whooshed from his lungs. "You're just visiting."

"So you *do* mind."

He did. A lot. Brady had a woman on his arm whenever opportunity afforded him the chance. Back in the day, he'd enjoyed using his role in the military to full advantage, to both impress women and as an excuse to lose touch. Now, he probably used his job's travel for the same purposes.

But Hale had no claim on Morgan. He'd just have to trust she was too level-headed to fall for him. "Let me know how it goes for you."

———

Morgan tilted her head at the unexpected word scrawled across one of Aunt Dorie's boxes. Toys?

Odd.

Aunt Dorie hadn't had kids, so she'd had no reason to collect toys in the first place, let alone save them. In the fading evening light, the painted metal trucks in the box looked at least fifty years old. Maybe more.

"Collectors would pay a pretty penny for those." The male voice behind her sent her heart tripping until her brain caught up with her ears. The pitch didn't belong to Hale.

The intruder from earlier stood in the opening of the garage door. His hair, in a ponytail, looked damp, but he wore the same purple T-shirt and jeans as before. He held up his hands, as if to put her at ease, but he grinned. "No need to call the cops again. We didn't get properly introduced, and I saw the light on over here."

Morgan leaned to see down the driveway. No Hale.

"I'm Brady. Hale and I served together."

"Ah." Bracing a hand on her thigh as she rose left behind a dusty print. The box must've been in storage for years. She brushed her hands as clean as she could. "Morgan."

"Pleasure to meet you, Morgan." Brady stuck out his hand.

Figuring he'd seen the dust and had offered anyway, Morgan shook with him.

He piled his other hand on, sandwiching hers in a more personal way than she'd anticipated. "Sorry about the scare."

She withdrew her hand. "It's Dax I was concerned about."

"Thanks for catching him. I know how hard that can be. Hale was the only one he'd come for at first. Glad to see becoming a pet hasn't dampened his spirit."

He'd said they'd served together, but she hadn't realized Brady would've witnessed Hale and Dax getting to know each other. He would've also witnessed other aspects of Hale's time in the military.

She shouldn't pry, but with a smile, he continued all on his own. "Took about a month of bribery for the rest of us to win Dax over."

"That's because he has good taste in people." Hale's voice cut through the darkness. He appeared beside his friend. Earlier, he'd dressed in a polo and dark jeans, probably trying to look his best for the Fieldings. Now, he wore athletic pants, flip flops, and a white T-shirt.

"That fits my theory too, since I was about to say that if Morgan caught him so quickly, Dax must be a fan of hers too." The full wattage of Brady's smile shone her direction. "He has good taste."

Was he flirting with her? This reminded her far too much of another Fielding, not classy Viv and her husband Mark, but one of Mark's brothers, Crawford.

She crossed her arms. "I suppose he does. Did Hale tell you how Dax introduced us?"

"No." His head cocked with interest.

She summarized the story. When she finished, Brady laughed loudly, and she found herself chuckling along until Hale's quiet attention on her served as a warning light. She pushed a lock of hair behind her ear and shuffled her attention back to the box of trucks. "You really think these could be worth something?"

Brady moved into the space beside her, and his arm brushed hers as he examined one of the vintage toys. "I'm no expert, but I'd guess fifty dollars each. Or more."

"Oh. Okay." So not enough to save the shelter. But then, as Hale had said, even pocket change added up. She accepted the truck back from Brady and sidestepped to put some space between them. "I'll look into it once I know why she had them in the first place." She held the truck so Hale could see it. "Did she ever get these out for you?"

Hale cut a leery look toward his friend before focusing on the toy and shaking his head.

"What's the story there?" Brady asked.

Oh, had she spilled another secret? She cringed her apologies to Hale.

"These belonged to Morgan's aunt. Morgan and I were friends as kids, so I spent some time with her aunt when she did. But . . ." He shook his head again.

"Whoa." Brady whistled. Or, tried to, anyway. The sound was mostly air with only a hint of a note. "So you two go even further back than we do."

Morgan opted out of a reply to avoid sharing more secrets.

"He acts all sensible and responsible now, but I bet he was a stinker back in the day." Brady bumped her arm again. "You must have some stories. I'd love to hear them over dinner sometime."

Her mouth dropped open, but she bit it shut again. Hale must not have told Brady about the kiss. Or, he had told him and had assured his friend what Morgan had been trying to convince herself of all this time—that it didn't mean anything. Couldn't mean anything.

Except seeing these two together highlighted the difference between Hale's personality—intense and determined—

and the more spontaneous fun seekers like Brady and Crawford.

While Hale glowered in the background, Brady's expression remained hopeful, a taste for amusement glinting in his eyes, even in the dim garage. Turning him down was like putting a puppy in his kennel.

"I work late most nights."

"Most nights, but not all?"

She gulped, forming a more straightforward answer.

Before she had to voice it, Hale spoke from beside her. "She's being nice. Don't make her spell it out."

She gave Brady an apologetic smile to confirm Hale's assessment.

"All right. Can't fault a guy for trying." He reached out as if to bump her shoulder but didn't actually make contact. "Besides, I'd say I owe you dinner after scaring you."

"And for letting the dog out." Hale's voice held a snap.

"And for that. So if you reconsider"—he took a backward step and tipped his head in the direction of Hale's house— "you know where to find me."

As his friend disappeared down the drive, Hale grunted. So he didn't like Brady hitting on her any more than she'd enjoyed it. But why? And did it matter? Or was she being foolish to think a connection with him was so different?

Morgan returned the truck to the box. "I feel like I keep telling your secrets. If I let on to something with Brady just now that you hadn't planned to tell him, I'm sorry."

"The fact that we knew each other as kids is as much your story to tell as mine."

Their shared history proved once more that, whatever their connection, it wasn't a spontaneous whim. At least, their friendship wasn't. She couldn't say the same about that kiss.

She snapped a picture of the toys so she could ask her parents about them. "He says you served together."

"Of course he mentioned that."

She took a couple of seconds to send the text, then slid the phone away. With the darkness growing ever deeper outside, the one lightbulb in the garage cast only a dim glow. The boxes swam with shadows, and her desire to continue working on the project ebbed. She motioned Hale out and closed the garage before joining him in the driveway. "Do you two not get along?"

"We do. He's just pretty quick to share facts he thinks will get him female attention."

So Hale had come storming up the driveway because he'd known Brady would hit on her. She dusted her hands together again and struggled to read the subtleties of his expression through the darkness.

He stepped closer. A little closer than necessary. "Look. I've been putting this off, but instead of avoiding it, we ought to talk about the other night."

She meant to make a sound of assent. The sound that escaped sounded more like she'd choked on a cough drop. If he was about to ask for a repeat, did she have the resolve to say no?

Negative.

Hale widened his stance and crossed his arms. "That probably shouldn't happen again."

Oh. Her shoulders, which she hadn't realized had stiffened in anticipation, relaxed. "Probably not."

Instead of accepting her agreement and moving off, though, he stood his ground. Creases in his forehead collected shadows. He had more to say. Maybe he was fighting the same battle as her, listing pros and cons. But in such an out-of-control world, love was too big a risk.

She stuffed her hands deep in her pockets. "I should get inside."

———

He'd gone and left her feeling rejected, when really, if he only considered her and the feelings she stirred in him, he wasn't sure he could maintain his long-held belief that a good relationship would eventually dissolve into chronic disagreement.

He liked her too much to let her disappear into her house without knowing the rest. As little as he cared to break the news.

He lifted his voice after her. "I'd be as bad as Brady if I let anything come of us."

She retraced her steps, head tilted. "How so?"

"Brady's looking for a casual date to pass the time while he's in town. He's staying long enough to help set up for Dog Days, but then he'll leave again."

"That's a difference, not a similarity." In this light, he couldn't make out the exact shape of her eyes. Judging by her voice, however, she'd narrowed them. She'd definitely locked her arms across herself.

"I'm thinking of going too. He offered me a job."

Her posture pulled straighter, and her hands fell to her sides. "You're leaving." She spoke as if he'd insulted her.

He understood. He never should've allowed anything to come of their connection. He just hadn't known the night of their kiss that Kerry could cripple his business.

"I haven't decided yet. I wanted to make a life here, but I need work, and one job for the Fieldings won't pay the bills. Brady's offering me a solid opportunity. And maybe . . . I haven't found what I was looking for here, and I have to consider that maybe I'm looking in the wrong place."

"Peace, right?" She advanced until she stood two feet away. "That's what you're looking for?"

"Between the Johanssons, Dax and Samson fighting, the shelter barely scraping by, and . . ." He pulled back from mentioning his feelings for Morgan. He couldn't bring himself to lump her with his problems when, near her, he felt more at peace than he had in ages. But this stage of the relationship wouldn't last. Pain would follow. Better to suffer it now, when it wouldn't be as bad. "Life here just isn't what it used to be."

"You're an adult now. You have adult problems. But it's still a peaceful place to live."

"Tell that to Kerry Johansson."

Morgan shook her head. "Jesus said He already gave us peace. If you don't sense it, maybe the problem is that you're trying to fight your own battles instead of trusting God."

His laugh soured in his throat. "You're one to talk. Seems to me you trust your plans a lot more than God with the way you run around trying to control everything."

"Not everything. Just myself. To be where I'm supposed to be, doing what I'm supposed to be doing." Her shoulders inched higher. "You might as well know, I was on a date when Aunt Dorie died. With a guy very much like Brady. And here I was just telling myself how different you are from Brady and Crawford, giving myself reasons to let loose and go for what I want for once. But you're leaving. Again. Because of course you are. Talk about a reality check. So really, thank you."

She'd packed so much into the rant, he didn't know where to start. She'd been out on a date. That would explain why she hadn't pursued a relationship any more than he had. Why she'd put up with his hot and cold attitude toward her. Still . . . "You don't blame yourself for Dorie's heart attack."

"No." She ducked her head, her breath loud in the quiet evening. "But I should've seen to my own responsibilities. If she hadn't been covering for me, her last night would've been at home, doing what she wanted, instead of at the clinic, covering for me."

"If she was at the clinic, she *was* doing what she wanted. She loved her work."

"Well, now I love it too." Spite dripped from her tone. "At least I know it's not going anywhere."

Unlike him—that implication was clear. "I'm not leaving to hurt you now any more than I was when I was thirteen."

"But you are leaving."

He scratched his scalp and shrugged one shoulder. His anger shouldn't make this decision for him. He'd meant only to warn her of the possibility, not to dictate a final outcome.

He wouldn't get to the life of peace he wanted through rash decisions.

He took a step backward. He needed to sleep on this. Cool off. Pray.

"You're running from your problems," Morgan said.

"If I go, it'll be a calculated choice I make because I do expect God to show up. He promised green pastures, and I'm not stopping until I find them. I'm just not convinced they're here."

"Right. Sure." She blew out a breath. Moonlight highlighted the ridge of her brow and left her eyes in deep shadow. She tapped her toe against the ground, nodded once, then turned and let herself inside.

Hale huffed through clenched teeth as turmoil roiled through him. So much time had passed since their childhood, yet here they were again. That was the trouble of trying to revive the nostalgia of his past. History—and not just the good parts—had a way of repeating itself.

fifteen

. . .

HOURS LATER, a screech pierced Hale's sleep. He fumbled for his cell on the nightstand to turn off the alarm. His hand hadn't reached the device when the rush of wind and rain against the house registered. Had a storm been forecasted?

He grasped his phone. The alert wasn't an alarm but a tornado warning. He usually kept a better eye on the weather reports because of how thunder affected Dax, but between Brady showing up, deliberations about leaving Chimney Creek, and Morgan, he'd forgotten to check.

Something crashed against the house. A tree branch? The maples on the property had been trimmed so only massive force could bend a limb far enough to reach the structure.

Dax licked Hale's knee.

"It's all right, boy. Come on." He silenced the alert and rose.

The whine of the tornado siren whispered between sheets of rain gusting against the house. The booms and flashes raged with fury that warned him property damage would be widespread. Already his bedside clock was dark, indicating they'd lost power.

Dax stuck close as he went downstairs. The interior front

door stood open, the glass of the storm door rattling as it held the gusts from sweeping the house. Brady stood out on the porch, shirt whipping in the wind. Hale opened the door just wide enough to slip out without allowing Dax any opportunity to bolt.

A flash transformed the night, then disappeared, thunder on its heels. Leaves and a plastic bag flew past.

Brady took a step backward, gaze locked on the sky like he was watching an alien ship invade. "That could be a funnel cloud."

Instead of verifying, Hale's vision locked on Morgan's house. Had she heard the alarms? The bushes on her property swayed like waves. Between their movements, light emanated from her basement. If his power was out, hers must be, too. Was that a flashlight?

"Yeah. It is." Brady grabbed his arm. "Time to get inside."

Hale cast a glance toward the sky. He couldn't make out a funnel cloud, but better safe than sorry. He followed his friend and Dax to the basement.

After they were closed in, Hale led Dax into the small room that had been used to store coal back in the day. The door had been removed from the closet-sized area before Hale bought the house, but the enclosure would provide more shelter than the open area of the basement. Brady followed and stood in the doorway, faced outward.

How was Morgan faring next door?

However angry she might be, he had to make sure she'd heard the warnings. He made the call.

She answered on the third ring, breathless.

"Are you in your basement?" he asked.

"Working on it. I can't find Patch, but once I—"

"Get in the basement now. Brady saw a funnel cloud."

In the beat of silence that followed, he imagined her freezing with fear.

"Morgan—"

"I'm going." And heavier breathing suggested she was going quickly.

Brady wandered from the coal room and craned his neck to see out one of the small, high windows. The view must not've told him much because he tried another.

On Morgan's end of the line, Hale heard a door open and close and a dog bark.

Brady wandered back. "Too much rain. I can't make out a thing."

"Okay," Morgan panted. "I'm in the basement."

"Hang tight until the warnings end."

They both paused at a crack and rumble. Had the tornado touched down? No, probably not. The noise didn't last very long. Then again, he'd heard tornadoes sounded like trains, and with the racket of the wind, rain, and thunder, he wasn't sure he'd hear a train.

Another explosion of thunder rocked the air.

"I'm not going anywhere," Morgan vowed.

"If you need anything, let me know." Expecting quick agreement, he shifted his grip on the phone, ready to disconnect.

"You're not going to stay on the line?" The question came quick and small. She was scared.

Though he'd taken cover, he wasn't. First, tornados in Wisconsin rarely did the kind of damage he'd heard of them inflicting in the plains. Second, even if this took a disastrous turn, he'd come to terms with his mortality years ago. If his time came because of this tornado, he had the peaceful green pastures of heaven to look forward to, same as everyone else who believed.

Another crash. A tree falling?

Brady darkened his phone and tucked it away, but in the next strobe of lightning, Hale caught his friend's look. Calm, but serious. If nothing else, there'd be a lot of clean up to do.

That part bothered Hale. The mess. The setback. The chaos.

Dax sank down next to him, apparently content, but anger that demanded an outlet collected in Hale's chest. No place was safe. No matter where he went or what he did, he had to fight battles.

His fighting days were supposed to be behind him. He wasn't in the military anymore. He'd gotten away from his warring parents. He'd safeguarded himself against the turbulence of romance. But he still had to navigate finicky homeowners, the shelter's dwindling finances, feelings he shouldn't harbor for Morgan, and now, nature's wrath.

Morgan had said he ought to have peace no matter what because of Jesus.

In a way, he did. He had peace about eternity. But what was he supposed to do in the meantime, when even creation seemed bent on waging war against him?

Maybe all of this was a sign. God wanted him to move on from Chimney Creek. Because life wasn't supposed to be like this.

"Hale?" Morgan asked.

"I'm here." For now. "I just don't have much to talk about."

"The storm can't last much longer, right?" Morgan asked.

"Right."

But so much damage had already been done.

———

Morgan woke covered in furballs.

Violet had curled up on the end of the couch, against Morgan's ankles and shins. The three cats, including Patch, whom she'd retrieved as soon as the tornado warning expired, had positioned themselves in the nooks and crannies around her. She could've returned to bed, but she'd decided to wait out the severe thunderstorm warning in the basement, too, so she wouldn't have to do another mad dash in the event it escalated again. She'd fallen asleep before the last storm warning expired.

But despite the fluffy company, she'd relegated this old couch to the basement for a reason. Its worn cushions and renegade springs hadn't been kind to her back or neck. She sat up, and two of the cats leapt to the ground. Only Blanca, purring, nestled closer as Morgan stretched her back and neck.

Sunshine angled through the cobwebbed windows of her unfinished basement. Rose and Violet pranced toward the exit, ready to go outside. She sighed, grabbed the robe she'd slung over her pajamas on her way down last night, and followed them upstairs.

She opened the back door, and the retrievers trotted out ahead of her. The roar of chainsaws obliterated the calls of birds, and as soon as her feet padded onto the patio, she drew to a halt.

The black walnut tree that formerly stood next door, opposite Hale's yard, lay across her entire backyard. The felled treetop reached nearly to Hale's garage, and its branches took up half of her yard.

The soggy grass squished underfoot as she investigated. Thankfully, no powerlines ran through the backyards, so there wouldn't be any live wires. The trunk had stomped her fence to the ground, ruining two lengths of fence, knocking others out of alignment. On the other side, the upper branches splintered, toppled, or crushed at least four more. Roofing shingles littered the grass. The limbs had torn them off the garage and gouged the underlying structure.

Violet and Rose ambled along the outer reaches of the tree, sniffing. With the fence compromised and the possibility that something sharp lurked in the yard, she hastened to call them away.

As she turned for the house, her line of sight swept toward Hale's. No trees grew in his backyard, but how had the two in his front yard fared? Hard to tell from here.

She sighed as she opened the door for the dogs. After their fight—knowing he was considering leaving again—she'd been silly to ask him to stay on the line with her, but his calm demeanor had ratcheted down her nerves. Weathering a storm with him had been . . . well . . .

Falsely reassuring.

He might leave, and the storm jeopardized their Dog Days plans, just days away.

A melody rose from her cell phone. She drew it from the pocket of her robe and answered. "Mili, any storm damage by you?"

"Some downed branches and powerlines, but mostly I'm worried about the shelter. I tried to drive out there, but the road's flooded. Would you and Hale try? Maybe his truck can handle the water, and if something has gone wrong, it'd be good for a vet to be there."

Great. Thrown together again.

If he was going to leave, the sooner he did, the better, because she wasn't sure how much time together she could handle. "Okay, it's early enough. I'll see if he can take me out before the clinic opens."

"I wonder how the park looks. Think they'll be able to set up the tents today?"

Morgan pushed her fingers into her hair and looked out the window at the fallen walnut tree. She'd considered that storm cleanup would give everyone more to do on their own property, but not the fact that the park would've been affected too. Enough downed trees would prevent the rental company from putting up the tents. That would push back other prep work for Dog Days, and then how would they get it all done? The schedule had been packed to start with.

More plans, out the window.

Hale's accusation echoed in her mind. *You trust plans, not God.*

Had he been right?

Maybe more than she'd wanted to admit.

Lord, I'm sorry. You promised to provide everything we need. Please do that.

She hung up with Mili, eyed her coffee maker, then decided she'd better use every second she had seeing to the morning's demands. There would be time for a sip of coffee between appointments once she got to the clinic.

―――――

As soon as Brady sliced a portion of the tree into a manageable size with the chainsaw, Hale hefted the piece into the bed of his truck.

Lightning had seared one of the maples in his front yard. A third of the tree had sheared off and damaged the porch's overhang, railing, and platform.

This would be an insurance claim, and he hadn't yet seen what the wind had done to the shingles on the roof. He could do the work himself, of course, but he might be busy. A storm like this would mean an influx of contractor work. Roofing and siding outfits from outside the area would likely swoop in for a few months, but that would leave structural jobs. Enough that locals couldn't be choosy. He'd likely get the chance to prove himself—and earn a living.

Assuming he hung around. He could take Brady's offer and earn a living that was less tied to a single place, less vulnerable to natural disasters.

"Hey, guys." Morgan's voice taunted him, as if to remind him that some of the trouble in his life, he'd brought on himself by falling for someone when he knew what that led to.

He threw a log into the bed of the truck and waited until it tumbled to a stop before turning toward her. "We'll start on the tree that fell in back when we finish here."

His attempt to act nonchalant failed him. She looked fresh and clean. Ready to tackle the day. Meanwhile, dust and sweat coated his skin and clothes. Yet, Morgan didn't crinkle her nose in disgust. In fact, she fell still, her face flushed, studying him.

The moment stretched. Her presence was like the calm in a hurricane. And maybe, with the way she looked back at him, she felt it too.

"You two need a minute?" Brady asked.

Hale tugged his shirt, unsticking the sweaty fabric from his torso.

"Mili called." Morgan's voice sounded high. Because of that moment—whatever it'd meant—or because of something Mili said? "She wants us to check on the shelter. She says the roads are flooded so she can't get there herself, but she thought your truck might make it."

"I don't know about his," Brady said. "But mine will."

To that, Hale had to shrug. His own pickup would get bogged down in little more water than it'd take to stop a car, but Brady equipped his truck for off-roading.

Morgan's irises flicked Brady's direction, uncertainty and perhaps disappointment shadowing her expression before she offered a glossy smile. "Okay. Is there room for three?"

Brady cast him a smug look, then laid aside the chainsaw. "I'll keep working here. Let me get the keys for the two of you."

Hale followed Brady in.

His friend swept his keys off the end table in the living room. "Treat her well." With that sly smile, Brady didn't mean the truck.

Hale shook his head. "Morgan and I aren't happening."

Brady smirked. "Remember the day I met Tanya?"

"You asked her out right in front of me."

"And you . . ."

"Laughed. She was engaged to me. I don't know what you expected to happen."

"I expected rejection a lot quicker than I got it. And when she didn't shut me down, I expected you to tell me off."

"So I'm not the jealous type."

"That was a good working theory until last night."

When Hale had hunted down Brady at Morgan's.

Brady lifted his eyebrows, a prompt for Hale to admit his interest in her. But he didn't object to a relationship with her because he didn't know his own feelings. He wasn't dating her because he'd decided not to. Because he wanted something different with his life. Eventually, his feelings would have to catch up.

"Your offer still stands?" Hale asked.

Brady's posture straightened with surprise. "The partnership?"

"If I'm going with you, I'm not stringing her along. But if you think that means I'll let you toy with her in the meantime, you're very wrong."

"You're really considering it?"

Hale extended his hand for the keys. "You came all the way here to talk me into it. You must've known there was a chance."

"I thought so. Then I met Morgan." Brady relinquished the keys. "I mean, like I said, I don't care if you bring her with, but does she want to go?"

"I'm more concerned with what I want. And you know what that is?"

"What?"

"Peace."

Brady's eyebrows twitched.

Hale didn't wait for him to comment. "So if you want me to leave Chimney Creek and go into business with you, when I say I'm leaning toward yes, instead of questioning me, you'll say, 'That's great.' Then, you'll leave me in . . ." He motioned for him to fill in the blank.

"Peace." Brady lifted his hands in surrender.

sixteen

. . .

MORGAN'S BRAIN had short-circuited when she'd seen Hale working in his yard a few minutes ago. The fact that the man possessed muscles shouldn't have been such a shocker, except she'd never before seen him put those muscles to quite as challenging a task as throwing around tree branches. Not that the visual was important, since he was leaving Chimney Creek, and by staring, she must have made him incredibly uncomfortable because he changed into a fresh shirt before rejoining her.

Apologizing would probably only draw more attention to her gaffe, so she bit her lips together and stared out the passenger window as he steered toward the animal shelter.

Chimney Creek had been hit hard by the storm. Each block seemed to have at least one downed tree. And then they passed the park.

She sucked a breath through her teeth. The little pond had flooded its banks, puddling to twice the size. Worse, at least a dozen trees had fallen, two or three of them quite sizable.

"Are we . . .?" Words failing, she pointed toward the problem. "That . . ." Tears wet her eyes. All those trees would have to be cleared before setup could begin, and the work would take all day. Or longer. Especially since anyone who would pitch in had their own homes to tend to. "Dog Days is too big to be rescheduled. We've done all that advertising . . ."

"It'll work out." But even his usually calm voice rumbled with frustration.

She leaned back in her seat and kept her mouth pressed shut. The next few days would not be fun, but the shelter hung in the balance. They had to do whatever the situation required to save it. If such a thing was still possible.

A few minutes later, they came to the flooding Mili hadn't been able to cross. Morgan's fingers tightened on the armrest. The standing water washed against the undercarriage, but Hale navigated through the low spot in a matter of seconds.

In another quarter mile, they would reach the shelter, but trees obscured it from view. She prayed it had survived unscathed.

"This job is a good opportunity," Hale said. "I'd be a partner in the business."

Really? He wanted to pick up the topic that had soured last night when they faced so many other difficulties? But once upon a time, she hadn't taken advantage of every opportunity with him. Whatever happened this time, she'd stay present until the end.

"There are good opportunities for you here too. You'll eventually repair the damage Kerry did."

His sigh said he didn't believe her but didn't want to argue. He nodded his chin and lifted a finger from the steering wheel. The rise where the shelter stood lay before them.

Relief mopped up some of the tension pooling in her midsection. "Still standing."

"Looks that way." Hale's tone warned her there could be problems they hadn't spotted yet.

He parked by the front door and left her to unlock it while he circled the building. He caught up with her inside, by the office. "The outside looks fine. No downed trees hit the building or the fences."

"No leaks that I can see in the office. Or out here." She cast another glance around the reception area, then they headed into the back.

The cats lounged as usual in their rooms, and the exam and grooming space appeared unscathed.

Hale's darkening expression mirrored her own concern, however, as they neared the dog kennels. Though the building had escaped damage, the storm seemed to have whipped the dogs into even more of a frenzy than usual.

Hale held the door for her.

No extra light peaked in through any new breaks in the walls or ceilings. She didn't spot any trickles or puddles of water either. And the lights worked. "All the racket must've worked them up."

Hale collected a handful of leashes. "Which ones would you say are worst? I'll take them to the outdoor play area and see if the others will simmer down."

Not a bad plan. Morgan walked the aisle, feeling like a prison warden assessing inmates.

She stopped at Samson's stall. Instead of the large Rottweiler, three smaller dogs jumped and pawed at the kennel door. "He's gone."

"What?" Hale reached her side, stared for a moment, then moved closer, as if he wouldn't have seen an escape route big enough for the one-hundred-twenty-pound dog from a step back. "Where is he? Did Mili move him?"

He stalked down the row. He must not've spotted the massive canine mixed in with the others, because he veered down the hall, probably to check the other rooms in the shelter. But Mili wouldn't have put Samson anywhere else. If she had, they would've found him when they toured the building for damage.

Morgan pulled out her phone and called her. "Where's Samson?"

"Oh."

She waited, but the director didn't continue. "What happened?"

"His owners saw the video we took of him for Dog Days. He wandered off eighty miles from here four months ago. They've been looking for him ever since but never thought he'd wander this far. Maybe somebody picked him up in between? They say he does have a chip, but it must've malfunctioned, since our scanner didn't pick it up. He was gone so long, they figured by now someone had found and decided to keep him. Once they realized we had him, they insisted I meet them after hours last night. They all came—a mom, dad, and their kids. Samson was really happy to see them. Ran straight up to them, wiggling like a puppy. It was the sweetest thing."

Morgan had witnessed many pets greet their owners. Even after a quick separation for a routine blood draw, the reunions could be sweet. As she pictured guarded Samson letting loose and charging his family with all the love his big heart held, moisture collected in her eyes. They'd found each other again despite terrible odds.

But their celebration meant separation for Hale, who'd become so attached, and that pushed her tears onto her cheeks.

"They paid all the fees and Samson's expenses," Mili said. "I have the money to give Hale back for everything he invested personally, but . . . um, well, I still haven't figured out how to tell him. I wish I'd thought of this before I asked you two to help this morning. The storm was just so bad that I didn't think of it. I'm really sorry."

Hale appeared again and splayed his hands, empty and questioning.

Heaviness settled in Morgan's bones. He wanted peace. Samson being ripped away from him would feel like the opposite. How could she tell him the dog he'd trained daily for months, the one he'd built a relationship with to adopt, was gone?

"How is everything there?" Mili asked. "Are the animals okay?"

"Stressed." She studied Hale, who could be described the same way.

He must've surmised Mili had given an explanation, because he watched her, still and intense. Braced like he could tell the news wouldn't be good.

She couldn't keep him hanging. She told Mili she'd call her back and hung up.

Hale's eyebrows lifted a fraction, and he crossed those strong arms of his.

In her practice, she sometimes had to give awful news. Fast and direct delivery usually served her and her clients best. "His owners saw the video. They reclaimed him."

His eyes darkened. "The people who made him so afraid?"

"He travelled eighty miles from home, and a couple of months are unaccounted for. Something must've happened during that time to make him afraid. Mili says he was extremely happy to see his people again."

"How could she do that? Just give him back. Without—" He bit off the end of the sentence, face taut with anger, frustration, and . . . grief? He ran a hand over his hair and stalked out the side door.

Morgan gave him space by circling back and checking on the cats more carefully. She refilled a spilled water bowl, mopped up the mess, and petted a few eager heads. Then, she returned to the dogs, who had calmed little. She picked the worst five and walked them one and two at a time to the play area. As she worked, she spotted Hale behind the building, sitting on a picnic bench with his back to the attached table. He had his elbows on his knees, his head in his hands.

Once she had the dogs settled, she sat next to him and ran her fingertips back and forth across the broad shoulders she'd spent too much time admiring this summer. "I'm really sorry."

He rolled his shoulders, shedding her touch, and leaned back, expression hard. "I'm going to work with Brady."

Disappointment stilled her. Though angry that his solution was to leave, she also hurt for him. The Johanssons had treated him unfairly, and she knew a thing or two about unexpected loss. She wasn't sure how to comfort him, so she prayed God would. Maybe that was one benefit to continuously finding herself in situations so far beyond herself—they forced her to turn again and again to God.

The dogs ran and sniffed in the enclosure, the stress of the storm now forgotten. If only Hale understood a simple change of scenery didn't transform a human as easily. Not when they carried their mindset with them. The irony was, Hale was looking for something he'd given her—only in bits and pieces, maybe, but nonetheless, she was grateful.

"It meant a lot to me that you stayed on the phone last night, through the storm."

His eyes narrowed.

With another prayer for help, she continued. "I know it's not what you wanted, but God's given you a gift for being a peacemaker. You did it for me during the storm. You tried to do it with Kerry, by not overreacting to her post. You succeeded with the committee, when I wanted to fight the plan to expand Dog Days. You gave Samson a lot more peace than he would've had too. And Dax."

He shrugged one elbow up to rest on the table behind him, frowning but listening.

"Maybe it's because you want peace so badly that you're so good at helping others to it."

"That'd be a cruel joke."

"It's a gift and a calling. And the Bible says God blesses the peacemakers. Don't get so busy working out peace in an external sense, that you miss the internal peace that comes from trusting Him."

"The whole point of moving here was to not miss it." With a single shake of his head, he stood and walked a couple of feet away, his back toward her. After a silence that stretched with as much heavy warning as a tornado siren, he said, "I'll finish the work I have contracted before I go. And rent the house out."

Loss coursed through her, so much like the day she'd discovered his empty house as a child. Back then, the decisions hadn't been his, but this time, he'd chosen, and he was running. If only she had something to offer to keep him here, but she couldn't loosen her grip on her veterinary practice again or who knew what she'd lose this time? Especially not when there was no guarantee the risk would convince him to stay.

He turned back to her. From beneath a furrowed brow, he scanned her and frowned harder at whatever he saw. "Let's get the dogs put away. You've got to get to work, and if Dog Days is going to have any chance at happening, so do I."

She nodded, numb.

The whole ride back into town, she strategized arguments to keep him, but nothing came. He'd come seeking peace, and even she had to admit more challenges than rest had met him in Chimney Creek.

He pulled to the curb in front of her house. Brady had cleared the fallen part of the tree from Hale's front yard, leaving the standing portion for another time. The drone of a chainsaw indicated he'd moved on to the walnut tree in back.

Standing beside the road, she held the truck door open

long enough to look back at Hale. "Promise me this time you'll say goodbye. That I won't just go over one day and find your place empty."

"I promise." Emotion roughened his voice, though which feeling affected him, she couldn't tell. Not regret, surely, or he would simply stay.

seventeen

. . .

HALE HADN'T SET out to coordinate storm cleanup for the entire town of Chimney Creek, but one thing led to another. He contacted committee members for help cleaning up the park. When a few of them said they first had to take care of pressing matters at their own homes and at the houses of those less able to take on the work, he'd offered himself and Brady to pitch in.

From there, word spread. People from church, the business community, and the high school organized teams and all called Hale for assignments. Likewise, residents in need of help contacted him.

Since he couldn't very well ask the community to support Dog Days if Dog Days didn't first see to their needs, he started two lists. Those with flooded basements and trees blocking driveways or causing problems in living areas he prioritized on one list, to be done before park cleanup. Those with less pressing concerns, like a downed tree that could wait a couple of days, he put on a second list and promised help after the fundraiser.

With six teams working around town and over a dozen projects in queue, he took more calls in one day than he'd received in a year, spam calls included. Somewhere along the line, he stopped bothering to look at the display before answering.

The phone rang again. He pulled off his leather work glove, swiped his thumb over the screen, and lifted the device to his ear. "Hello?"

Silence.

"Hello?" He started to lower the phone to look at the caller ID after all but then heard a voice. He pressed it back to his ear.

The caller described a tree that had fallen on the back of her house. "It hit the kitchen window. You know, the one facing north, and Fletch of course, is no good with any tools."

At the name Fletch, Hale pieced together the identity of the caller. Kerry Johansson had come to him for help. Morgan might've called him a peacemaker, but if he'd checked the display, he would've let this call go unanswered.

But Morgan also labelled his role as a peacemaker a *calling.*

And now an opportunity had literally called him.

Conviction stirred. Earlier today, as he rode with Brady to one of the work sites, he looked up the verse. It promised that peacemakers would be called children of God. This identity, and not the resolution to his conflicts with people, was the reward. The only thing that truly mattered was his standing with the Lord. He needed to remain faithful, even when things weren't going his way.

"I've heard the only way to get any help is through you," she finished.

According to the Bible, kindness toward an enemy would pile heaping coals on their head—which probably wasn't meant to condone a vengeful attitude. For now, he'd do what he knew was right and pray God would help his heart to follow his actions.

"I'll add you to the list. Since it came into the living space,

I'll get someone over there today to make sure it's sealed against the elements until your contractor can fix it permanently." He struggled to keep bitterness from his tone.

She hesitated, thanked him, and disconnected.

"Who stole your sunshine?" A log thumped into the trailer next to him.

Hale added the Johanssons' house to his list, pocketed the phone, and turned to resume helping Brady load up the logs others cut and tossed their direction. "That was the homeowner I was telling you about."

"The one who's running you out of town?" Brady lifted another log.

"If that was her goal, she's getting her way."

Brady paused, the log still in his grip. "She is?"

"Yeah. I'm in. I'll wrap up my responsibilities here and take your offer."

Brady whistled—a skill the guy had never mastered—as he tossed the log onto the pile and turned for the next. "I was just thinking, I finally get it."

"Get what?"

Brady waved a hand through the air, like their surroundings made the answer obvious.

Hale wiped his forehead with the back of his wrist. The crew had made quick work of the limb that had fallen across Edie's driveway. Now most of the group was eating casserole off paper plates.

"I don't follow."

"Chimney Creek." Brady pushed back hair that had fallen from his hair tie, only for it to fall right back. "I get why you like it here. One frustrating homeowner aside, it seems like they need you here."

"Someone else would've stepped up if I wasn't here."

"Maybe. Maybe not. It's pretty rare for a community to do this much for each other, and you get something from it too.

Coordinating all this. Your mood was actually better there for a while."

Maybe it was.

Blessed are the peacemakers.

But he wasn't sure he could credit his mood to the beatitude. He'd been encouraged by the prospect of saving Dog Days by working through the list. Aside from Kerry, that wasn't exactly peacemaking.

Now, he wondered if all the effort would pay off. If people kept calling all day to add projects, their volunteers might be too exhausted by the time they finally made it to park cleanup.

Brady rested his hands on his hips. "Don't tell me you've become the kind of guy who can get derailed by a little storm."

"This little storm might spell doom for the animal shelter, and trying to save it was the one thing in my time here that seemed to be working out."

"That and Morgan."

"We don't want a relationship. Let it go."

Brady released another log into the trailer. "Look, I don't want to talk you out of working with me, but these things happen everywhere. Storms, nasty customers, hurting charities. Working with me, you might even see more of it than you do here. Travel shows you both the good and the bad, if your eyes are open. Yours usually are."

Was that the key to happiness? Ignorance?

Breathing hard from the exertion of stacking logs, Brady spared him a glance. "In this world, we will have trouble, remember?"

Hale remembered, all right. He hefted the next log off the ground.

"But take heart. Jesus overcame the world." Brady paired the Scripture paraphrase with a cheesy grin.

If Jesus overcame the world, why did the trouble have to

continue? But then, faith meant believing in things he couldn't see. So was that the answer, then? To trust God, despite the trouble? To stop looking for peace and just accept the way things were?

That didn't sound right. Jesus said He gave His followers peace. So where was it?

Brady eyed him as though he could tell their talk hadn't helped. Apparently at an end of his resources, he motioned Hale toward the house. "Go eat."

As if a casserole would make him feel better. But Edie waved him over, and Hale went. The peace business—both finding it and making it—was hopeless, but he could at least make Edie's day by visiting for a few minutes.

———

"How have they been doing this all day?" Hannah stabbed her fists against the small of her back and arched her spine.

Morgan attempted to blow a lock of hair off her forehead, but it stuck to the sweat clinging there. "I have no idea."

They'd begun helping with storm cleanup after finishing work just forty-five minutes ago, but many of the volunteers scattered throughout the park had been undoing storm damage since morning. Hale led the charge, but he hadn't used his scheduling duties as an excuse to avoid hard work himself. He and Brady worked on the other side of the park's pond.

The set of their shoulders might've been a little lower than normal, and Hale's jeans and T-shirt both had tears that hadn't been there this morning, but the men continued to saw and stack logs with power Morgan couldn't dream of dredging up.

"He's always been a force to be reckoned with, hasn't he?" Hannah stooped to gather more brush.

Morgan followed suit, collecting sticks under her arm to

tie into a bundle. "He won't be ours to reckon with much longer. His friend offered him a job. He's leaving."

Stationed next to the stick Morgan reached for, Hannah's sneakers froze in place. "What?"

Morgan tied a bundle and deposited it in the wheelbarrow. "His friend offered him a job, and he's not happy here, so he's going."

"What about you?"

"What about me?" As if she wasn't already tired enough, her body grew as heavy as her mood. "We had . . . a moment, I guess, but it's not like I've ever been his deciding factor."

Suspicion narrowed Hannah's eyes. "A moment?"

Morgan retreated into their assigned task.

"I want details." Hannah's footsteps swished in the grass behind her. "I can't believe you'd keep something so big from me."

Before she spilled her secrets in earshot of the whole town, she scanned their surroundings. Nearby, a few teens raked, but they were caught up in their own chatter and games.

"It wasn't big. It was one kiss." Her inhale carried the scents of chainsaws, fresh-cut wood, and damp air. "We may have thought we fell for each other, but Hale's not one to stick around. Besides, romance isn't in the plan, remember?"

Hannah regarded her with a humorous glint in her eye so long that Morgan once again returned to work.

Hannah's hands appeared next to Morgan's, snatching up more brush. "You could change your plan. I mean, planning seems like one of Hale's strengths, so I'm sure you could figure out a new one together."

"Yeah. Except he's leaving like people are prone to do." The words cut like thorns pulled from deep in her flesh, a wound she didn't usually let herself think about too much.

Hannah stilled.

Morgan did too, because her body was on the verge of betraying her, threatening not just sniffles and tears but a full-blown breakdown. People she loved left. First Hale. Then her parents. Then Aunt Dorie. Now, Hale again.

How had she been so blind as to give him this power again?

"Hon." Hannah smoothed a hand across her back. When Morgan didn't straighten and face her, she dropped to her knees and peered up into Morgan's no-doubt splotchy face. "I'm so sorry you've been hurt."

Morgan lowered to the grass. Sitting was less weird than standing bent over like she was collecting sticks when her arms weren't moving. She rubbed her forehead and breathed deep and slow.

She'd tried safeguarding herself with plans that tied her to just one person, a person she'd trusted to stick it out. But then Aunt Dorie died, and Morgan clung all the tighter to her plans. She'd pulled back from Crawford and even distanced herself some from Hannah. And she'd never given Hale a real chance. Which, at this point, was for the best.

"Does Hale know you feel this way?"

That depended on what part of it she meant. Hale knew she didn't want him to go. He couldn't know how deep her abandonment wounds went, because she'd just put it all together herself.

"You have to tell him. If you want to truly connect with anyone, you have to be real. Risk being vulnerable."

She already *was* vulnerable. Too vulnerable. All the time, in ways she never imagined. Whose best friend just left without saying goodbye? Whose parents up and moved across the country?

"The alternative is living more or less alone."

"That's the plan."

"I say this with all the love in my heart, but that plan is a bad one."

It was all she had.

"It's unfair to claim Hale isn't one to stick around,"

Hannah said. "Last time, he didn't have a choice about leaving."

He'd had a choice about *how* he'd left, though. Morgan kept the argument to herself. He'd promised to say goodbye this time. She trusted him to follow through.

"Maybe he needs you to give him a reason to stay. Your work is important and maybe love would require adjusting your plans some—not as much as you act like, mind you. Don't you think the gain would be worth the change? I mean, if you love him. If you don't, that's another thing. But if you do and you walked over and told him so, I'd be shocked if that alone didn't convince him to stay."

"You're oversimplifying this." Still, Morgan tracked children chasing each other across the park lawn. It wasn't that she didn't like the idea of a family, in theory. And even Aunt Dorie had found time to make a difference to the children in her life. Was Hannah right? With the right man, could she find a way to balance career and marriage? A family?

"Only one way to find out." Hannah motioned toward Hale.

Go tell him she loved him?

Was that even true?

She'd certainly come to depend on him with the committee. She respected his service to the country, and she loved his heart for Dax and Samson. His calm confidence had reassured her during the storm. His work ethic would save the shelter if anything could.

Chimney Creek wouldn't be the same without him.

Hannah elbowed her arm.

Going and giving her heart to a man with an exit strategy already in motion would be asking to obliterate the remains of her already broken heart. She wiped her face, rolled her shoulders, and stood to resume her work. "We're not meant to be."

"Okay. If you're sure." Hannah climbed to her feet with a

groan and rubbed her thighs. But instead of complaining about the obvious soreness, she reached for the next stray stick.

Morgan had filled a bundle and was securing it with a string when Hannah nudged her and pointed.

Kerry and Fletch Johansson entered the park. Fletch, a big guy who'd been a linebacker in high school, carried two rakes. Next to him, Kerry wore old jeans, a T-shirt with a restaurant logo, and a bandana tied over her hair.

"A little late," Morgan mumbled.

Everyone else who'd received help from Hale's crews today had already been at work in the park for an hour or more. Even Edie had come, serving drinks and fresh cookies at a card table she'd set up in the parking lot.

"There's still enough to do." Hannah waved a greeting.

Fletch split off and joined a group by one of the larger fallen trees. Kerry continued to Morgan and Hannah's wheelbarrow.

"We came to help." Kerry hooked her thumbs into her back pockets and shifted uncomfortably. "Do I need to check in with anyone in particular?" Her line of sight seemed to flick to Hale, then dropped toward the collection of sticks.

"Nope. Just pick up sticks." Hannah offered a friendly smile.

Morgan forced something meant to look similar and pushed the wheelbarrow to the truck that would take the bundles to the yard waste site. When she returned to Hannah and Kerry, they had three more bundles waiting. Morgan hooked her fingers under the string of one, but it'd been tied loosely, and the sticks spilled across the grass.

"Oh. Sorry." Kerry knelt to join her in picking up. "You and Hale are close, right?"

So they were going to have to talk about it. She measured her anger against Hale's dedication to handling the situation well and tailored her response accordingly. "We're neighbors. Why?"

"Well, because . . ." She paused as if retying the bundle took all her concentration. When she finished, she put the load into the wheelbarrow and crossed her arms. "I doubt he'd come back to finish our remodel if I asked, but maybe if a friend of his did, he'd consider it."

She couldn't be serious.

But she squinted at Morgan as though she was.

Across the pond, sawdust flew around Hale as he braced against the pull of the chainsaw to guide the blade through a tree trunk. No wonder Kerry didn't want to go have a difficult conversation with him right now.

All the better, because it meant Morgan got to field this one for him. Maybe he was leaving, and yes, that hurt incredibly, but well, maybe she did love him. "I thought you were unhappy with his work."

"Our new contractor quit. Apparently, I have impossible demands, and I'm impossible to work with." She waved a stick around, a rather dangerous time to talk with her hands. "He wouldn't match Hale's prices or his timeline—the adjusted ones—and Fletch refuses to invest more in the project budget. He says I've either got to get Hale back, or I'll have to choose cheaper materials. The whole point was to have my dream kitchen, so going cheap defeats the purpose."

So she wasn't sorry for the trouble she'd caused.

"You were one of his first projects in town. After you made such a big deal of firing him, others backed out of working with him. He doesn't have enough jobs anymore."

"So he'd be willing to come back, you think?"

Where was this woman's sense of responsibility? Morgan would like to shake her. She'd settle for lecturing her. But she was only having this conversation because of her friendship with Hale, and he was a peacemaker. And what if Kerry could give him the reason to stay that Morgan had been unable to muster?

What if he stayed?

She couldn't say what might happen between them, but she wanted him in Chimney Creek. Badly. Even if they never did end up together.

"I honestly don't know what he'll do," Morgan said. "But if you help him regain some of what he lost, I'll talk to him."

"How would I do that?"

She pointed to some of the homeowners who had cancelled projects. "Talk to the Lees and Aaron Billings about how Hale did quality work at a competitive price. If they rehire him, I'll let him know who put in a good word for him."

Kerry studied the other homeowners. Finally, she nodded and set off across the park.

"Well, that's an answer to prayer," Hannah said once she'd gone.

An answer to prayer, and a reason for Hale to stay.

But would it be enough?

eighteen

. . .

HALE WATCHED Kerry making the rounds. How much more damage did she think she could do to an already dead reputation? He started his truck. Just a little longer, and he could head home to a hot shower, his dog, and the couch. And in a few weeks, he would be done with this town altogether.

Brady secured a tarp over the load and gave a thumbs up. Hale eased the truck forward, conscious of the soggy grass. The clean-up efforts would leave ruts crisscrossing the park, but they'd made enough progress. Tomorrow morning, they could set up the tents, and then they'd have to jam the rest of the preparations into the afternoon and evening. With this many hands to help, they could pull it off.

Maybe he *was* a peacemaker.

Now if only God would play that role for Hale.

The streetlights in the park flickered on as he pulled onto the road. Only then did he spot Morgan crossing the park toward his parking spot. She stopped short. Had she been coming to talk to him? He braked, but she turned away and rejoined Hannah. Must not've been important—if she'd been looking for him at all.

He continued to the Chimney Creek resident who'd agreed to take this load of wood to stock his wood-burning stove. By the time Hale and the homeowner finished piling the wood beside the garage, Brady texted that the last load had left the park. His work for the night finished, Hale drove home, bone tired.

Once he parked in the garage, he collected his work gloves, keys, and water bottle, and hopped out of the truck.

"What if someone wanted you to stay after all?"

So Morgan *had* been looking for him. New energy warmed his aching muscles. He met her in the driveway. "Who's the someone?"

"So that's a yes?" With dirt and grass stains on her jeans, she looked more like the adventurous girl he'd once known than she had since he arrived. He wished he could slip the tie from her ponytail, setting her hair free around her shoulders. "You'd stay if the right someone wanted you to?"

He would be tempted if Morgan asked, and the shy way she couldn't hold his gaze suggested that might be on the table. He shouldn't encourage her to put herself out there like that after he'd given his word to Brady. But he also couldn't quite bring himself to close the door on the possibility of hearing her say they were worth fighting for.

A smile ghosted her features. "Kerry wants to rehire you so badly, she spent the night convincing the Lees and Aaron Billings and one or two others, I think, to hire you back. To undo the damage she did, so you'll reconsider working with her."

So Morgan didn't want him to stay. His nemesis did. But surprise tempered his resentment. He walked with her to the porch. "What changed her mind?"

She dropped into one of the chairs and pulled her feet up onto the seat. "Your prices and timelines can't be beat. The new guy quit on her."

He laughed, satisfied. But then something in him—the

Holy Spirit, probably—told him not to be so petty. To rethink how this fit with the bigger picture. With the fact that he'd asked God to act as his peacemaker.

Kerry coming back around—and winning back some of his customers—was a powerful answer to that prayer. He'd grown tired of fighting, so he'd stopped, and here God had won the battle for him.

Or was he reading too much into it? Rubbing his face, he shook his head. He'd definitely asked. And that made this one of the clearest answers to prayer he'd ever gotten. He laughed again, satisfied on a completely different level.

"Kind of funny, right?" Morgan asked.

"Striking, anyway."

He'd taken the smallest step in faith by treating Kerry with the same kindness he'd extended to others. God had multiplied that beyond his expectations into a gift, an undeserved reminder of His provision. Into a blessing.

He wished he hadn't sacrificed so much peace along the way, offended by his circumstances, disheartened by his trials. Instead, he could've trusted and stayed the course, bypassing unnecessary angst with faith that God would keep His promises and work all things for good. He recommitted himself to making better choices moving forward.

Morgan studied him, hope clear in her blue eyes. "Does it change anything?"

Kerry's change of heart reopened his career prospects. But it was his own change of heart that would finally enable him to enjoy the green pasture God had plopped him down in months ago.

"It changes a lot." He opened his hand to her.

She hesitated and the indents by her eyebrows deepened.

His perspective had changed; hers hadn't. Still, reluctantly, she threaded her fingers with his, their hands suspended between their chairs.

He drew a deep breath. "It's a sign that God is exactly Who you said He is."

"Who's that?"

"Our Peacemaker. I've been asking Him to show me the path to peace for a long time." He paused, reflecting as connections lit up. "It was waiting right on the other side of surrender."

"I suppose that's how a lot of things work." Her words came haltingly, towing heavy ideas behind.

Did she realize what all this might mean for them? If God was his peacemaker, and Hale kept learning to work with Him better, his own marriage could be different than his parents' strife-filled one. His search for a peaceful life could be satisfied in decades of evenings like this one, debriefing with Morgan after a full day's work.

But for that to happen, she'd have to surrender some ideas of her own. He turned her hand. With the sun below the horizon, the streetlights sent a glow across her skin.

"So you'll stay?" she asked. "Since your career is back on track?"

"Is that why you want me to stay? My career?"

She licked her lips but didn't answer. Not verbally. But her choice to slip her hand from his told him plenty. "Answered prayer and your job are pretty good reasons."

"True, but I was hoping for one more." He'd stay regardless of her response, because the most important factor was one she hadn't listed: he sensed he was where God wanted him. But living next door to Morgan would be bittersweet if she kept her heart behind a much more effective fence than the one surrounding her yard. He had to try laying it all out for her. "I like you, Morgan. I'd like to pursue this. See what the future holds."

She locked her arms across herself as though suddenly cold.

The storm had brought the temperatures down. He rose. "I'll get you a jacket."

"It's okay." She stood, too, a sad smile tugging her lips. "Home's right next door."

He'd planned to run away from his problems, too, so he understood the impulse. He also understood that he'd done his part, and the rest was up to the Lord. At least she wasn't going far, and for the God who'd brought down so many barriers to peace in his own life, her little fence wouldn't be any problem at all.

———

The following morning, set up for Dog Days kept Morgan's body busy but left her mind woefully free to remember conversations from the day before. Hale hadn't exactly said it, but she suspected he was staying. The next move belonged to her: trust him enough to allow him into her plans, or keep herself as safe as possible by following Aunt Dorie's example.

She stuck blue tape on the pavement, marking the divide between one vendor's assigned space and the next, then measured off another twelve feet. She left two more T's made of tape at the front and the back of the space.

Hale rolled lengths of orange safety fencing to encircle the agility course, and when their eyes met, he smiled as though he hadn't offered his heart only for her to walk away.

She tore the tape, completing another T, but the roll got away from her and skipped across the asphalt. She groaned and chased it, hunched like an old man trying to retrieve his hat from a renegade breeze. Before her fingers closed on it, the roll bounced against a woman's sandals.

Morgan lifted her gaze to find a familiar face smiling down at her.

"Mom!" She straightened and wrapped her in a hug. "What are you doing here?"

Stepping back, her mom held her shoulders and studied her face. "This is a big event for you, and would've been for Dorie too. We wouldn't miss it."

"We?" She scanned the park and found her dad helping set up obstacles in the agility course. "Wow. Thank you. I'm glad you're here."

Mom tweaked her shoulders, then swept up the tape and offered it to her. "How can I help?"

Morgan passed her the tape measure but held onto the end herself. "Let me know when I've gone twelve feet."

Her mom did, then joined her as she started applying the tape. "You asked about the toys you found in Dorie's things. I've been meaning to answer."

"Oh. You know?" Morgan tore off a piece of tape.

"Well, I don't know for sure, mind you, but I do know the trucks have been handed down through your father's family. So my best guess is, when their parents downsized, Dorie stored the toys away in hopes of letting her own kids play with them one day. When she never ended up having a family, maybe she didn't have the heart to get rid of them. Or she could've forgotten she had them—maybe wouldn't have even remembered if she'd had the kids she wanted so badly." Mom chuckled warmly, as if the idea that Dorie could've forgotten about a box of trucks was the most important part of what she'd said.

Morgan rocked back on her heels and peered up from where she squatted. "Aunt Dorie wanted a family?"

"Well, of course, sweetie."

Of course? She finished marking the spot, and Mom gave her a hand up. "But she said getting married and having kids wasn't in the plan."

"Apparently, it wasn't." Mom's mouth pulled into a wistful frown.

"I'm so confused."

"It was *definitely* in Dorie's plan. But that's not always the kind of thing a person can decide for herself."

"Then what did she mean when she said it wasn't in the plan?"

"God's plan, maybe?"

Morgan reconsidered the years of conversations she'd shared with Aunt Dorie. They'd discussed Morgan's love life, the demands of vet school, Aunt Dorie's retirement plans, and so much more. How had something so significant not come up?

Her mom handed her the end of the tape measure to mark off the next spot, but Morgan couldn't move. "It isn't possible."

"Honestly, I'm not sure it would've been for me to accept singleness the way she eventually did. My marriage and kids mean the world to me." Her eyes gained a sheen, and she forced a helpless smile. "I don't understand why God didn't give her that. But I believe with my whole heart she's surrounded by all the love and family she could ever want now."

Morgan released a watery sigh of her own, overcome by both the heartbreak of unfulfilled longings and the joy of being united with a family more real than anything Earth had to offer. "She never explained. How could she never have said anything?"

"She wasn't one to complain. Besides, she had you and your siblings. And Hale, too, for a while. But you were special to her. I think she was least likely to mention wanting family to you because, in you, she felt like she had a daughter. I was jealous of your connection with her from time to time, especially when you asked to stay with her instead of moving with us. I refused at first, remember? But your father and I talked at length, and it was what you really wanted. In a way, maybe that prayer of hers was answered after all." She tweaked Morgan's elbow.

She opened her mouth, but what could she say? She hadn't remembered her mom refusing to let her stay in Chimney Creek. But she had protested, hadn't she? That realization alone was healing. Her parents loved her. Their departure wasn't an abandonment, even if it was a separation. Really, most of her losses could be labelled that way, as a departure rather than an abandonment. Hale's first move away and Aunt Dorie's death certainly could be. Add to that reassurance her new understanding of Aunt Dorie's dreams, and maybe her own plans could afford to change.

"Anyway." Mom brightened her expression and wiped under her eyes. "I didn't mean to pull down the mood. I simply suspect that's why she had those toys. You can do whatever you'd like with them. And look at us." She laughed down at the tape measure they still held. "Standing around gabbing like there isn't work to do."

"Right." Morgan forced a laugh and pushed herself into motion. It was a wonder she could walk a straight line with how fast her mind spun. Aunt Dorie would've jumped at the chance for a family of her own. She would never want Morgan holing up with plans in favor of pursuing love, especially since Hale was staying.

They had a real shot now.

But how in the world would that look?

"That's twelve feet," Mom called.

She stooped with her tape and made a T while her mom approached. "Do you think Aunt Dorie could've still run the clinic the way she did if she'd had a family?"

Mom's sandals scuffed to a stop nearby. "Maybe not quite the way she did. She had a lot of love to give, and since she didn't have her own family, she poured a lot into her clients and her business. But she still could've been a successful vet and a business owner. Life takes balance, is all."

Balance.

Aunt Dorie had wanted a family. Life took balance, and her plans, it seemed, had tipped a little too far toward ideas she hadn't really understood. She'd have to surrender them to God, see how they could be rewritten. Which was kind of Hale's specialty.

nineteen

. . .

THEY'D FAILED. Morgan blinked at the totals from the auction and tried to hold back tears. Would Hale still stay if the shelter closed?

"How'd we do?" His voice came from over her shoulder and echoed in the cavernous park shelter.

When they arrived back after church, Mili asked for his help in the adoption tent, leaving Morgan alone to add up the amounts from the auction.

Not trusting her voice, she slid the paper toward him. His footsteps slowed beside her, and she heard the quiet pat of his hand settling on the back of her chair as he read the outcome of all their work.

"Not awful," he said.

"Not good enough either." She avoided tilting her head up to make eye contact, but she could feel his attention settle on her.

"We did well," he insisted. "This will keep the shelter going another eight or nine months, and we can use that time to raise the rest."

"Except you're not staying." So, yes, she'd stooped to baiting him. She wanted him to stay. She suspected he planned to. And yet, instead of just asking, she went and said something like that.

His hand shifted to her shoulder, warm, and she could hear a smile slant through his voice. "If I go, you get to go back to doing things your way. That wouldn't make you happy?"

Not in the least. Without him, the whole thing seemed hopeless. She couldn't imagine how far short they would've fallen without his vision. With him, she'd actually enjoyed coordinating the extravagant event. Mostly.

"Hey." He knelt beside her and looked up into her face.

She rubbed her forehead, but she couldn't hide from him forever. Finally, she lowered her hand to her lap.

His blue eyes peered up at her, deep with reassurance and kind understanding.

She choked out her real hangup. "I know in my head that changing my plans is for the best. I want to be another reason you stay. But I've spent a long time thinking that sticking to the plan would keep me safe."

The corner of his mouth lifted with the makings of a smile. "The way things worked out with Kerry showed me God's better at arranging things than I've ever been. If He's a peace-maker for me like you said—and He is—He's also an excellent planner for you."

Hale moving in next door had been God's plan. Dog Days too. And though she didn't understand some of her losses, having notice and being able to plan for them wouldn't have made things much better. She'd still be finding her way without Aunt Dorie.

Was it also God's plan for her and Hale to end up together?

"I'm staying, no matter what you choose." He brushed her cheek. "The question is, which is stronger? Your love for me or your hate for change?"

She smoothed a hand onto his shoulder. "I'd be a fool to pick hate."

His eyes flicked, taking her in. A grin spread across his face. "I love you too."

His joy was contagious. And maybe the sentiment too. "You do?"

He rose and tugged her hands until she joined him. "I'm not going anywhere."

The promise was salve to hurts she'd had so long, she hadn't even realized how they limited her until now, as they healed over, one conversation at a time, one layer after another. "I love you too."

"Then the first change I propose is that I can kiss you whenever I want." He shifted closer, his gaze lazily perusing her lips and then rising to await her response.

"That sounds like a change I could live with."

He lifted his hand to her neck, and his thumb caressed her cheek as he sealed the agreement with a kiss. For more moments like these, she'd hire a second vet. Plus, the broad shoulders beneath her hands would help carry the weight of responsibility, and she could help encourage and support him too. Together, they could have all kinds of adventures.

Instead of feeling like her whole life was more or less planned, a course she only had to follow along its inevitable path, she now saw possibilities. And the joy those possibilities brought her only made the kiss all the sweeter.

An unfamiliar chuckle registered. "Excuse me."

At the woman's voice, she pulled back from Hale. He cut Morgan a look meant, she suspected, to remind her they'd agreed he could kiss her whenever he wanted. But then a deep-throated bark turned their attention to the visitor—a visitor with a giant black-and-tan dog at the end of the leash she held.

The Rottweiler tugged toward Hale. The woman might be slight, but she wasn't a pushover because she managed to moderate Samson's pace so he didn't plow into Hale. He did, however, close the gap.

Hale released his hold on Morgan just in time to greet the dog.

"Samson?" Morgan looked to the woman for confirmation. It certainly looked like the rescue.

The woman was tall and slender with her dark, wavy hair in a pixie cut. Small stud earrings ran up the edge of her right ear, the one thing about her that glittered, contrasting with the casual style of her black T-shirt and jeans. "Bubba, actually. We let our kids name him."

Morgan turned her attention back to the happy reunion. Samson didn't seem to know whether he wanted to stand close enough to be petted or to tear off in search of a toy to wrestle Hale for. Even on his best days at the shelter, he hadn't been this joyful.

Neither had Hale. He laughed and scrubbed the dog's ears.

"You must be the one who spent so much time with him," the woman said.

Samson slouched to the floor and rolled belly up, waiting for a rub.

Hale complied as he glanced up at the owner. "He's a special dog."

The woman nodded. "To us too. I'm Erin, by the way. We were devastated when we realized one of the kids accidently left the door open and he'd run off. After a few days, we didn't think we'd ever get him back. I can't tell you how grateful we are that he found his way to someone who looked out for him the way you did."

As if to testify to his contentedness, Samson relaxed on his side as Hale ruffled his fingers through his fur. "I was grateful to know him, too, but I heard he was excited to see his owners again." After one final pat, Hale rose, as if distancing himself from what he couldn't have, and settled his arm around Morgan.

Seeking attention, Samson—Bubba—pushed up onto his feet and trotted back to Erin. "My husband and I would like to thank you for what you did for him."

"Oh." Hale shook his head. "Not necessary. I'm glad I could offer him a little peace in the storm."

"I like that." She studied Bubba a few beats and nodded, as if coming to a decision. "When we picked him up, Mili told us everything you did for him. She said you hoped to adopt him yourself. My husband and I talked it over, and the breeder we bought Bubba from will have another litter available in a couple of weeks. We'd like to purchase one of them for you as a token of our appreciation."

Wow. The going rate for a purebred made the offer generous.

But Hale shook his head. "I appreciate the idea, but that's not necessary."

"Maybe not, but we'd like to thank you."

"If . . ." He hesitated, seeming to weigh his options. "If you're that grateful, you could consider donating the money you would've spent on a puppy toward the shelter. Even after this event, we're short on operating costs we need for the coming year."

"Oh. By how much?" Erin had reclaimed the leash, and she shifted it from one hand to the other so she could pull her cellphone from her back pocket.

Morgan let Hale be the one to name the amount, figuring the woman would be disappointed that even a contribution that matched the price of a purebred wouldn't close the gap. But when Hale gave the number, she simply nodded.

"Any little bit would help," Hale said. "If you're willing."

"Absolutely." Erin passed Bubba's leash to Hale and stepped toward the door. "Let me chat with my husband, and I'll see what we can do."

———

Hale resisted getting back down on the dog's level as Erin stepped outside. It was good to see him, good to get closure, but letting him go again would be even harder if he enjoyed this brief reunion too much.

Morgan's fingers ran up and down his triceps. "I'm proud of you."

"For what?" For how ridiculously attached he'd gotten to this dog? He sighed.

"For putting the shelter's needs above your own."

He shrugged one shoulder and allowed himself to pat Bubba's head. "It wouldn't be practical to have two dogs of my own right now. I've already got Dax and you have Violet and Rose. A three-dog household is probably full enough without a one-hundred-thirty-pound Goliath ambling around."

"Did we get engaged and I missed it?"

"Not yet." He kissed the side of her head. "I figure you're only game for one change at a time, and for now, I'm still pretty pleased with my first choice." As if to prove it, he dipped his head for another kiss. When he pulled back, he drew her into a one-armed hug. "But I've got peace about this."

She snuggled closer. "Me too."

epilogue

. . .

DAX'S BARK, crisp on the snowy afternoon, drew a smile to
Morgan's face. She snagged the mail from the box by her
front door and hurried to the back so she could catch Hale
before he and Dax went inside.

In theory, they saw plenty of each other. Hale's days had
filled with contracting jobs, a combined result of the
Johanssons changing their tune and of Hale proving himself
to the community with his storm cleanup efforts. His online
reviews spoke so highly of him, he had homeowners from
neighboring towns contacting him about their projects. But he
stuck to what he and the small team he'd hired could handle
between eight a.m. and five p.m.

Morgan, too, had limited her workdays, even though it'd
meant turning over the care of some of her old regulars to the
new vet she'd brought on staff. That whole thing still made
her shake her head.

One Friday evening, after a particularly long and stressful
week, she lamented to Hale that she'd never find someone to
help in her practice. She'd already been looking for months.
He'd prayed with her about it.

A week later, in walked Chase Poplin, fresh out of vet

school, looking for a chance to prove himself. He considered working the later shift a bonus, since it meant he got to sleep in, and he did his job with pep she envied. The practice was in excellent care when she left each evening.

She and Hale cooked together, walked their dogs, and dreamed up new efforts to help the shelter. Although she wasn't so sure God really needed their help, since He'd done so much more than she'd dreamed.

Turned out Erin starred in a successful car repair show, and her husband drummed for a famous rock band. Their donation filled the gap in the shelter's budget. So, the pressure was off, and fundraising planning had become a fun part of their peaceful evenings.

Despite seeing Hale plenty, the sight never got old. Maybe she could steal a kiss over the fence before she went in to feed her dogs. Dax continued to bark, the rascal. It was unlike Hale to let him go on this long, but maybe he'd stepped in the house for something.

She let herself through the gate and into the backyard. Dax, once more on her side of the fence, trotted through the snow to her, tail wagging.

"What are you doing here?" She scrubbed her fingers against his neck, grateful for his warmth. She should've pulled on gloves, even for this short trip to the mailbox.

At least this time, Dax hadn't pulled the tie-out right off the house. But Hale wouldn't have let him loose, so . . .

She glanced at Hale's house. She didn't see him, but her fingers brushed a container attached to Dax's collar. What in the world?

In her attempt to reach the red box despite Dax's squirming, she bumped it open. A coin-like object sank into the fresh layer of snow covering her patio, followed by a small roll of paper. She snatched both up before she lost track of them in the snow.

Instead of a coin, she opened her fingers to find a ring.

She glanced up in time to see Hale clear her fence, as agile as ever, despite his boots and winter coat. Dax ran to him as Morgan unrolled the paper.

Marry me?

Her breath caught, and she clutched the ring in her freezing hand as she watched Hale approach. His posture remained as confident as ever, but he didn't seem sure he ought to smile.

After everything they'd been through, surely he knew what her answer would be.

She straightened and lifted the note. "Is this you or Dax asking? Because my answer will change, depending."

He took her hand and lowered to one knee. He must've found the reassurance he'd needed in her expression, because a smile edged his eyes, joy banked and ready to shine. "You are my shelter in the storm, Morgan Reynolds, and I want to be that and so much more to you. Will you marry me?"

She nodded, on the verge of choking up, but she couldn't cheat him out of his answer. "Yes, Hale. I'll marry you."

He slid the ring on her finger, and his smile took over, transforming the face she'd thought, on their reunion, so serious. Intense around the eyes. As he rose again, those same eyes glinted with the boyish mischief that had drawn her to him when they'd been young.

He looked like exactly what he was—an adventure waiting to happen.

She pushed up on her toes to kiss his cheek, but he intercepted her, claiming her lips instead. Just one more change of plans in what had turned out to be a glorious string of them.

———

The Lord is my shepherd; I shall not want.
He makes me lie down in green pastures.

He leads me beside still waters.
He restores my soul.
He leads me in paths of righteousness
for his name's sake.
Psalm 23:1-3, ESV

A sweet small-town romance exclusively for Emily's email subscribers.

Food trailer owner Asher has seen too many tears he couldn't dry. Determined to be part of the solution, he avoids romance and all the heartbreaking drama that comes along with it.

At least, that's the plan until his heart decides it has a mind of its own. If he can't rein it in, he's destined to break not one, but two women's hearts.

Sign up for email newsletters at emilyconradauthor.com and receive *Between The Two of Us*, the prequel novella to the Rhythms of Redemption Romances, as a welcome gift.

author's note

Dear reader,

While Dax and Hale are purely fictional, non-profits that help reunite soldiers with pets they bonded with while serving overseas are real! If you're interested in learning more, one organization to check out is Paws of War (https://www.pawsofwar.org/war-torn-pups).

I hope this story has been something of a green pasture to you. I don't know whether you could use a peacemaker, a planner, or something else entirely, but I do know God is enough to meet our every need.

Thank you for picking up *On The Fence About You*. Your support in reading, reviewing, and sharing about my books helps make it possible for me to continue writing them, and your friendship and enthusiasm makes it fun.

May the Lord lead you to green pastures.

Emily

also by emily conrad

The Rhythms of Redemption Romances

To Bring You Back

An Awestruck Christmas Medley

To Belong Together

To Begin Again

To Believe in You

The Many Oaks Romances

Now or Never

A Surefire Love

A Faithful Protector

Christmas in Redemption Ridge

Bidding on a Second Chance

Matchmaking the Cowboy

Risking His Heart

acknowledgments

I started this story in 2020 before the lockdowns and finished the first draft just a couple of months later. When my initial plans for this story didn't pan out, I set it aside to focus on The Rhythms of Redemption, but it's so good to get to circle back to it now and share it with you.

For help with this story my thanks go out to: Amy Renaud, Maria Thouron, Jessica Bradley, Jane Bradley, and Kendra Arthur. I'm grateful for the time and care you gave this story.

Thank you, readers, for venturing to a new town with me. I hope you spend happy hours here.

Thank you, Lord, for the green pastures You've placed me in. May my life bring You glory.

about the author

Emily Conrad writes contemporary Christian romance that explores life's relevant questions. Though she likes to think some of her characters are pretty great, the ultimate hero of her stories (including the one she's living) is Jesus. She lives in Wisconsin with her husband, an energetic coonhound rescue, and two lop-eared bunnies. Learn more about her and her books at emilyconradauthor.com.

facebook.com/emilyconradauthor

instagram.com/emilyrconrad